'Why don't y… misery and j… do for you?'

He swallowed, shifting his weight until it was evenly distributed on both shiny new riding boots. 'Ms Somervale, my name is Ryan. Ryan Gasper. I am Will Gasper's brother. I know it is a long time coming, but I have come in response to your letter.'

Laura watched in stunned silence as in seeming slow motion he then pulled a crumpled piece of lavender notepaper from the pocket over his heart and held it towards her.

'I have come to find out if what you wrote in your letter is true. Are you the mother of Will's child?'

Ryan Gasper, Laura repeated in her mind. *Wannabe cowboy, city gent, heaven-in-a-pair-of-blue-jeans is Ryan Gasper!*

'Ms Somervale, I'm not here to cause you or your...family any trouble. I've come because...'

Why had he come? To find the child she had written to his parents about in her letter? Absolutely. But after that he was running on gut instinct alone.

Having once been a professional cheerleader, **Ally Blake** has a motto: 'Smile and the world smiles with you.' One way to make Ally smile is by sending her on holidays, especially to locations which inspire her writing. New York and Italy are by far her favourite destinations. Other things that make her smile are the gracious city of Melbourne, the gritty Collingwood football team, and her gorgeous husband Mark. Reading romance novels was a smile-worthy pursuit from long back, so with such valuable preparation already behind her, she wrote and sold her first book. Her career as a writer also gives her a perfectly reasonable excuse to indulge in her stationery addiction. That alone is enough to keep her grinning every day! Ally would love you to visit her at her website www.allyblake.com

Recent titles by the same author:

THE WEDDING WISH
MARRIAGE MATERIAL
MARRIAGE MAKE-OVER
HOW TO MARRY A BILLIONAIRE
A MOTHER FOR HIS DAUGHTER

A FATHER IN THE MAKING

BY

ALLY BLAKE

MILLS & BOON®

To my friend Mel, for a trillion different reasons, with an extra hug thrown in for the loan of the gorgeous view from the corner of her desk way back at the beginning of all of this.

First published in Great Britain 2005
Paperback Edition 2006
Harlequin Mills & Boon Limited,
Eton House, 18-24 Paradise Road, Richmond, Surrey TW9 1SR

ISBN 0 263 84874 4

Set in Times Roman 10½ on 12 pt.
02-0106-50988

Printed and bound in Spain
by Litografia Rosés, S.A., Barcelona

CHAPTER ONE

RYAN pulled off the winding country road onto a long gravel driveway and slowed his car to an idle. A weathered wooden sign at the turn read *Kardinyarr*. He looked to the return address on the letter laid flat on the passenger seat of his car. Youthful handwriting on lavender stationery, dappled with fairies, smudged with tears, scrunched into a ball, and flattened again, told him that this was the place. Kardinyarr was where he hoped against hope to find her. Though she had written the letter several years earlier, Ryan had only stumbled upon it that week, and it was all he had to go on.

He gunned the engine, his tyres skipping and jumping over the uneven dirt track. He slowed again as a family of grey kangaroos bounced at the same pace along the other side of the neat wire fence, before leaping onto the road, hopping in front of his car, and bounding up the rise to his left and disappearing over the other side of the hill.

'Well, that's not something you see every day,' he said.

Ryan ignored the 'Private Road' sign at the first gate and drove up the hill. At the fork in the drive he pulled left, coming to stop under a sprawling banksia tree in the front yard of a rambling brick home.

The CD of a keynote speech he had given at a recent economic summit in London, an addendum to a university-level economics textbook he was in the final stages of editing, came to a sharp halt as he switched off the car engine. His mind otherwise engaged, he had barely heard a word of the familiar oration on the two-hour drive from Melbourne, but the deep well of silence that now filled the car was deafening.

So this was Kardinyarr House; the last home his little brother had known. Backlit by the light of the setting sun, proudly situated atop its windy hill, it was just as Will had described it all those years before. A black corrugated roof and matching shutters framed the clinker brick. A neat veranda laced with black wrought-iron trim hugged the house, rendering a pretty finish to the sturdy structure.

Ryan's recent hasty research told him it had been left vacant in the years since Will's passing, the foreign owners of the property keeping the acreage as an investment rather than an operating farm. As such, Ryan had expected scattered leaves, debris on the veranda, and obvious decay. However, the place seemed neat and tidy. Maintained. Welcoming.

Will had e-mailed the family when he had first arrived at Kardinyarr.

There is no place like it. The colour, the light. The fresh air gets under your skin.

Ryan opened the car door and took in a deep breath of clean country air. Will had been right. There was nothing quite like the mix of scents bombarding him—sweet pollens, swirling dust, and hazy country heat that seemed to have a scent all of its own. The acrid smell of car fumes that he'd left behind in Melbourne faded to a memory.

'Okay, Will,' Ryan said aloud. 'It's charming here. I

get it. But so charming as to shoulder out all other options in your life?' Ryan shook his head.

Kardinyarr was meant to have been a brief stop on Will's winter backpacking trek around the country. But from the chain of information Ryan had uncovered in the last few days he believed that if his brother had not been killed, he might never have left at all. All because of the girl in the crumpled lavender letter.

Ryan grabbed the offending document, folded it carefully, and placed it in the top pocket of his shirt. He hopped out of the car, instinct causing him to lock it. A wry smile tugged at his mouth. He hadn't seen another living soul for five kilometres, bar the kangaroos and a half-dozen cattle standing under the shade of a wide-branched gum. *You can take the boy out of the city…*

The pleasant breeze tickling at his hair dropped suddenly, and he heard a noise coming from the other branch of the gravel drive. Opera. It had the sharp scratchy timbre of a record, and in the now still air it carried past him and beyond, echoing in the gullies either side of the hilltop. He swished a buzzing fly from his face and looked to the broken wooden gate that had long since been swallowed by lily pillies, climbing vines, and a lush Japanese maple.

On the other side of that gate he hoped to find the woman who had written that long-ago, tear-smudged letter. Perhaps she could tell him why his infuriating little brother had been offered the world, and refused it.

Laura's head bounced up and down in time with the music.

She loved days like these: a little cloud cover to take the edge off the summer heat, but not enough to stop the differentiation of light and shadow playing across the

Kardinyarr hills. Once she had hung the washing, and finished dinner, she had a slot in her evening for a too hot bubble bath. The very thought had her happy as a kookaburra!

The record player was turned up loud enough to create a hanging-out-the-washing soundtrack. She hummed along with the orchestra and sang aloud in makeshift Italian to the magpies lined up on her roof gutters, tragic operatic hand movements and breast-thumping included. Okay, so she was no Pavarotti, but what did the magpies know?

Enough, it seemed, as soon they skedaddled, flying off in muddled formation to land in a gum tree further along the hill. 'Come on guys!' she shouted. 'You'll usually put up with a great deal when you know there's honeyed bread in it for you!'

The song finished, another began, and Laura went back to her chore. She grabbed a heavy white cotton sheet and lobbed it over the clothes-line, thinking she would teach them a lesson. 'No honey on your bread today. So there!'

Ryan pushed his hands deep into his jeans pockets as he walked up the gravel drive.

Once, Will had e-mailed their sister, Sam.

I have never felt so alive. You guys have to come out here. You have to come and see what I mean. Only then will you understand why I plan to stay.

But they hadn't come. They had all been too busy. His sister Jen as first violin of the Sydney Symphony Orchestra. Sam with her young family and her self-funded quilting magazine, with its monthly worldwide readership in hundreds of thousands. And his parents, wildlife documentary film-makers, who spent all their time in faraway jungles.

Within a fortnight of that e-mail having been sent, Will had been buried back in their home town of Melbourne. It had been a drizzly winter's day, with a hundred people watching over him—or so Ryan had later been told.

Past the broken wooden gate and atop the short rise, a small transformed worker's cottage came into view. Multi-coloured flowers bordered the full-length portico, trying desperately to cling to life in the dry conditions. A water tank sat rust-free against the near wall. The fence was neat and the grass was short, but in need of rain. And through the white sheets flapping on the old-fashioned circular clothesline, Ryan caught sight of an ambiguous female form. *Laura Somervale.*

What would she be like, the woman for whom Will had given up an Oxford scholarship? Would she be quiet and bookish? Would she be artistic and soulful? Or would she simply be a girl? A country girl who had caught the eye of a lonely, mixed-up, directionless city boy? Would life have worn her down, or would there still be a glimmer of the girl with the fairy stationery? What sort of woman could make a Gasper turn his back on all that?

Some kind of woman, Ryan thought sardonically, for here she was, doing it again. She had drawn him out of his perfectly civilised world of five-star hotels and nightly political debate over cocktails, and into her world of dirt and heat and flies, with a page of tear-smudged words written many years before.

The circular clothesline turned and Ryan glimpsed a flash of sun-kissed auburn curls.

She's adorable. And sweet. She makes me laugh. She makes me feel ten feet tall. This is her home, and, as such, it feels like my home too.

A wry smile crossed Ryan's mouth. Will must have known exactly the response his realist big brother would have given to such poetic musings; which was why he had never let Ryan in on the exact nature of his feelings about the girl he'd met at Kardinyarr. Will had saved the deep and meaningful outpourings for their sister.

'Adorable' Ryan didn't need. Answers. Information. Reason. Those things he could tie off in a neat, contained system, once he'd closed the page on the question still buzzing in the back of his mind after all this time. *Why here, Will? Why?*

As Ryan neared, he realised that the woman behind the flapping white sheet was singing…almost. Occasionally the notes coming from her and the notes coming from the speakers matched, but due more to random luck than skill. It was unabashed, full-tilt, and indescribably terrible.

He slowed. Perhaps he ought to have called first. Meeting her like this would be like talking to someone with parsley caught in their teeth. Did you mention the fact and embarrass them? Or ignore it and pretend it wasn't there? As Ryan tussled with his decision, the woman pulled herself around the heavy damp sheet until she was revealed fully to him, and he couldn't have switched direction if a bushfire had sprung up between them.

Auburn curls twirled long and thick down her back, tied into a low loose ponytail with what looked like a pink shoelace. The setting sun shone straight through the cotton of her simple floral sundress, highlighting a long-limbed, youthful figure hidden beneath.

The wind picked up, whipping from out of the gully at the rear of the property and across the hilltop. It was enough to knock Ryan sideways, but the woman's feet remained steadfastly planted as she reached up to peg a pillowcase to the line. The wind blew about her knees, the thin fabric of her dress clinging to her. Her curling ponytail flapped in a horizontal line before sinking into a thick wave down her back when the wind settled.

She bent down to gather another sheet, one bare foot kicking out behind her for balance. As she came back upright she returned to full voice, head thrown back, hips swaying as the music reached a blazing crescendo.

'Now, how do you like that, Maggie?' she called out, turning on the spot, arms outstretched, her dress spinning high revealing a pair of smooth, tanned legs.

This was Laura Somervale? This vivacious creature was brooding Will's mystery dream girl? This happy-go-lucky woman had written words of honest, tear-drenched pain and longing to a family she had never met?

It was suddenly too much. What had he been thinking of, jumping in the car with nothing more than an over-night bag and cannon-balling out to the middle of no-where to find her? He should have used her example and written.

He stepped backwards, but the crunch of his riding boots on the gravelly earth sounded loud in the now still air. Like a hiker who had stumbled upon a scorpion, Ryan stopped still with one foot cocked against the ground.

The woman spun from the hips and stared him down with eyes the colour of the creamy-gold grass at her feet.

The afternoon sun shone into her face, casting a glow over her naturally bronzed skin. And, since his breath had long since escaped his lungs, Ryan said nothing as he returned her silent stare.

Laura held up a hand to shield her eyes from the setting sun as she looked over the stranger who had wandered unexpectedly onto her small patch of the world.

All thoughts of Pavarotti and too hot bubble baths slipped from her mind to make way for a pleasing combination of tight, dark curls and eyes as blue as the wide-open sky above. The stranger's shoulders were broad enough to carry a bale of hay, his long legs were encased in taut new denim, and strong muscled forearms appeared below the rolled-up arms of a new chambray shirt. There was even something faintly familiar about his steady blue gaze but, considering all the other visual enticements on offer, she couldn't put her finger on it. Either way, the gent was so nicely put together he could have been a poster boy for country living.

But parked under the banksia tree in front of big, beautiful, empty Kardinyarr House next door, was the gent's car. She had been singing so loud she hadn't even heard it arrive. The car was black, sporty and expensive, and covered in fresh dust. The dust made her smile. No matter that he wore the local uniform, and wore it extremely well, this guy was no local. Clothes too new. Car too flash. Haircut too neat. He had city boy written all over him. Laura was a born and bred country girl, so it was unlikely this guy had ever meandered through her life before.

So who is he? she wondered. Some lost tourist looking for directions? Or a strip-o-gram organised by Jill, her friend and resident busybody? Ha! If only!

Nah, he's a salesman, she decided. In that flash car,

with those trying-to-look-like-a-cowboy-clothes, he was equipped to charm his way into selling something to somebody. She then noticed the length of the stranger's shadow. Whatever he was selling, the sooner he was gone the better. The tiny window she had later in her day, time in which to soak in that too hot bubble bath, relax, maybe even read a chapter of the thriller that had been collecting dust on her bedside table, was slipping away the longer she dilly-dallied.

'Hello, there,' she singsonged.

He gave her a short nod, tipping his hand to an imaginary hat as he did so. *Ooh, too smooth.*

'Am I interrupting you?' he asked. His voice fitted the rest of him to perfection. Persuasive, elegant, and deep as the gully slipping away behind him.

'It's probably best you have,' she answered. 'Or I would never have had all this washing on the line before the sun sets.' *Hint, hint. I'm a busy woman with no time for salesmen, devastatingly handsome or otherwise…*

'You weren't talking to someone?' he asked, missing her point as he looked past her to find the elusive Maggie.

Her grin turned to a grimace. To be caught singing was one thing. To be caught talking to the birds was quite another. Living atop her beloved hill, she had been without daily adult contact for far too long. 'Only the magpies,' she admitted with a shrug, but naturally they had not remained in sight to prove her tale.

His deep blue eyes crinkled at the edges, hinting that a decent smile played thereabouts on occasion, but no smile creased his handsome face just yet. 'Do they talk back?'

'Not in so many words,' she said. 'But we have an

understanding. They listen to me sing and I thank them with food. Honeyed bread is their culinary preference.'

'Ah, so you buy their affection?'

'It seems to be the only way I can get any nowadays.' *Oh, Laura, did you seriously just say that?* 'Any audience willing to listen to me sing—Puccini in particular,' she qualified. 'Not affection. I get plenty of affection without having to pay for it.'

Just shoot me where I stand, please, she begged anyone listening in to her thoughts. The intent gleam in the stranger's intense blue eyes had her gabbling. Or maybe it was the fact that most of the guys around those parts were wizened, bow-legged, and married, and this one seemed to be a very nice combination of anything but. Then again, perhaps it was the still distant possibility that the guy was a strip-o-gram that had her in a flap. *What the heck?* she thought. *I have the music going if he has the moves!*

Ryan was speechless. An in-demand public speaker, he modified the thinking of powerful people every day: politicians, special-interest groups, people a lot bigger and scarier than this auburn-haired spitfire.

Sweet? This woman was a heck of a lot more interesting than plain old sweet. Her eyes told the tale before she even opened her mouth—she was direct, sassy, and visibly attentive. But, then again, perhaps this wasn't Laura Somervale. Absurdly, Ryan's pulse quickened at the theory that perhaps this was a complete stranger, some glorious, undiscovered creature he had chanced upon all on his own.

And then he remembered the inflammatory letter burning a hole in his shirt pocket. Oh, this was she. This creature with her bare feet and tumbling curls was the girl who had spilled her broken heart onto girlish lavender paper. *Now who's being a poet? Come on, smart guy, stop delaying the inevitable and fess up,* his conscience implored. *Just tell her who you are and what you know.*

The woman's feet caught up with her hips as she turned fully to face him, and he saw that her spare hand gripped a set of little girl's pink overalls.

The words in the lavender letter, which until that moment had seemed somehow unreal, crystallised in that moment. A little girl. Ryan's heart thundered so hard his ears rang from the blood-rush. She had a little girl.

'So, now that you have been witness to me embarrassing myself on several levels,' the woman said, 'I'm sure you can find it in yourself to tell me what you're doing here.'

'I came by way of Tandarah,' he said, evading the question, needing the extra time to control his breathing again. 'The woman who runs the Upper Gum Tree Hotel sent me here.'

Suddenly the strip-o-gram fantasy was not nearly so ridiculous after all. Laura felt her cheeks warm. She even had to clear her throat. 'Jill Tucker?' she said. 'Short silver hair? Mischievous gleam in the eye?'

The man nodded. 'She sent me up here as I'm looking for Laura Somervale.'

Well, if he was a salesman he was exceedingly customer-specific. Laura dropped the hand shielding her eyes long enough to swish it about, presenting herself to him like a prize on a game show. 'Well, now you've found me what are you going to do with me?'

When he didn't answer straight away, simply watching her with that relentless, memorable blue gaze, Laura did as she was wont to do when faced with an unsettling silence. She stumbled in with both feet a-tapping.

'Have I won the Lotto?' she asked. When he still didn't flinch, she blundered on. 'No? Well, I don't need aluminium siding on the house, I only buy the local weekly newspaper, and I am perfectly happy with my long-distance phone plan—especially since everyone I know lives hereabouts.'

His slow blink proved he was selling none of the above. But a curious smile kicked at the corner of the wannabe-cowboy's lips. Just as she'd expected, it was an engaging smile, a tempting smile, and a smile that gave her heart-rate an entirely satisfying kick.

Laura changed her mind about the salesman angle and decided her run of bad luck had ended and God was offering her one big, juicy payback in the form of a dashing man. Instruction sheet attached—feed three square meals a day, does have expensive tastes, but likes to give back rubs and draw too hot bubble baths three times per week.

'Now, this has been a fun way to spend the last few minutes,' she said, 'but why don't you put me out of my misery and just tell me what I can do for you?'

He swallowed, shifting his weight until it was evenly distributed on both shiny new riding boots. 'Ms Somervale, my name is Ryan. Ryan Gasper. I am Will Gasper's brother. I know it's been a long time coming, but I have come in response to your letter.'

Laura watched in stunned silence as in seeming slow motion he pulled a crumpled piece of lavender notepaper from the pocket over his heart and held it towards her.

'I have come to find out if what you wrote in your letter is true. Are you the mother of Will's child?'

Ryan Gasper, Laura repeated in her mind. *Wannabe cowboy, city gent, heaven-in-a-pair-of-blue-jeans is Ryan Gasper!*

Her mind went over all fuzzy, as her memories skipped and tumbled back through the years to the last time that name had been foremost in her mind…

She stood, sheltered, hidden by a weeping willow, a good twenty metres behind the congregation at the edge of the cemetery, feeling like Alice gone through the looking glass.

In her pale pink sundress and her borrowed tweed coat, her pink headband holding back her mass of curls, which had gone wild in the drizzly Melbourne weather, she felt out of her depth, like a kid playing dress-up, hoping the adults wouldn't notice she didn't really belong.

The hundred-odd people huddled together against the cold were a who's who of the Australian social set. Even she, a girl from the bush, recognised the multitude of television personalities and politicians alike. They were all dressed up in glamorous black, in hats, in designer sunglasses. The only hat Laura had ever owned was a twenty-year-old Akubra of her father's, bumped and bruised by years of wear while working the land.

Standing apart from the throng, she clutched a letter in her cold hand: a letter laboured over, cried over, written longhand, on stationery she had received a couple of years before on her sixteenth birthday. Fairies danced in the top corner of the page and hid behind toadstools along the bottom rim. She hadn't really paid attention when writing on it; she had only given in to the burning need to get her despairing words onto paper.

She rested a protective arm across her flat belly. It would not be flat for much longer. Talk between the young mothers in Tandarah came back to her. Stretch marks. Bladder problems. Varicose veins. She was eigh-

teen, for goodness' sake! How had her life turned so completely in the last two months that she had ended up here?

But what choice did she have? What with both her parents gone, these people were the only family her child would know—this overwhelming, well-to-do, influential, formidable group of people standing watching over the casket of heavy wood that contained their son, their brother.

Through gaps between the sea of black coats, Laura watched as the casket slowly sank into the rain-drenched ground. From nowhere, the disturbing strains of a solo violin wafted over the gloomy scene, and her heart grew so heavy with sorrow she could barely breathe.

Will. Dear, sweet Will. He had been so unassuming. So gentle. So uncomplicated. One would never have guessed that he came from such a family. But in the last few days she had found out the truth of it. She had read the small notices of condolence in every newspaper in the country. Devoured them. Clipped them and kept them in a precious shoebox beneath her bed back home. Somehow it had helped her live outside of herself, outside of the poignant realisation that she was pregnant, and that the father of her unborn child had been killed before he even knew.

Laura made an effort to place as many of the mourners as she could—anything to take her mind off the weight in her heart. The violinist had to be one of the sisters—Jen. The younger of the sisters, Samantha, was very pregnant herself, and married to a television actor. Will's parents, the elegant couple standing either side of the minister, were award-winning film-makers.

But where was the elusive elder brother? The one Will talked about more than the rest. Ryan. The workaholic perennial wanderer, the oft-published, world-renowned economist who travelled the world at the whim of foreign governments in order to advise them on economic policy. Will's hero.

The family moved forward, each to throw a blood-red rose atop Will's coffin, but no young man came forward with Will's sisters and parents. As far as Laura could tell, illustrious big-brother Ryan was not there.

She had come this far, catching a bus, a train and a tram, alone, to get there, to be present when her young friend was lowered into the ground. Ryan Gasper had the means, the money, and the time. How could a man not move heaven and earth to be at his own brother's funeral? And how could Laura bring her only child into a family such as that? So scattered. So civilised. So impenetrable.

Laura looked to the letter in her hand, now crunched into a tight ball in her shaking palm. She smoothed it out again and slipped it deep into the pocket of her borrowed coat. She would post the letter on the way back to Tandarah, and then it would be up to them to make the next move.

'Until then,' she whispered, her words forming a cloud of steam in the chill winter air. 'I think it's fair to say it's just you and me, possum.'

Eighteen years old, and all alone in the world bar the tiny speck of life inside of her, Laura turned and walked away without looking back…

Ryan watched Laura's warm, open face slowly crumble and turn paper-white. She didn't move, didn't blink, and didn't even seem to notice when the pink overalls left her limp hand and fluttered to the dusty ground.

'You're *Will's* brother?' she whispered, her previously

chirpy voice now thin and faraway. Wisps of dappled hair had fallen from their restraint and curled across her forehead. Without all the bluster and noise she suddenly looked very frail. Delicate. And terribly young. He took a step her way, for fear she might swoon.

'Ms Somervale?'

She made no move, as though she had not heard him.

'Laura? Are you all right?'

When she swallowed, her lips trembled. Then her haunted gaze locked in on the letter in his still outstretched hand. Her hand flew to her mouth and her teeth clamped down on the length of her index finger. Ryan knew not if she was stopping herself from crying out or biting down hard to cover up a deeper pain elsewhere inside of her. And then, just when Ryan was about to reach out and gather her against him—anything to stop the unnerving trembling that he had caused—she did the incredible: she managed to muster up a smile.

'You're Will's brother,' she repeated, and this time it was a shaky statement, not a question. 'Ryan. The economist, right? I'm sorry I didn't recognise you. Will never did carry pictures of any of you. And you weren't at his funeral.'

Did that mean she had been? He'd had no idea. His family must not have either. Astonishing. She had been in their midst all those years before, and none of them had known. 'Ms Somervale, I'm not here to cause you or your…family any trouble. I've come because…'

Why had he come? To find the child she had written to the Gaspers about in her letter? Absolutely. But after that he was running on gut instinct alone.

He reached down slowly, so as not to startle her, and picked up the pink overalls. 'I need to know, Ms

Somervale.' He handed them back to her and saw understanding dawn upon her face.

She took a great breath, as though gathering her scattered trains of thought, nodded, and her bottomless golden eyes fluttered back up to meet his. 'The Upper Gum Tree,' she said, coming out of some sort of trance. 'The hotel in town where you met Jill Tucker. Six o'clock tonight.'

Before he even had the chance to ask her what made the Upper Gum Tree at six o'clock so special, a voice called out from deep within the cottage.

'Mu-u-um!'

'Coming, possum!' she called back, her flashing eyes begging that he keep his attention on her and nowhere else. But it was a hopeless demand as suddenly the owner of the pink overalls and the shouting voice came skipping out of the cottage.

The crackling record, the whisper of the breeze, even the vibrant vision of a barefoot Laura Somervale slipped away as every ounce of Ryan's being focused on the little girl. She had Laura's oval face, healthy glow, and dishevelled curls. But the Gasper traits were unmistakable. The intelligent blue eyes. The square jaw. Even the way she bit at the inner corner of her mouth was a habit his sisters had never overcome.

There was no longer any doubt in Ryan's mind. Laura Somervale had given life to his brother's child.

The little girl was holding a crayon drawing in her hand, and she stopped short when she saw that her mother was not alone. 'Mum?' This time her voice was not so resolute.

Laura's glance flicked towards the little girl, her voice neutral. 'Go back inside, Chloe.'

Chloe. Ryan spun the name around his mind several times. *Chloe Gasper. No, surely not. Chloe Somervale.*

'Get Chimp's dinner ready. I won't be long. Okay?' No matter that she was trying desperately to sound all right, they heard the strain in her voice. Chloe nodded, and looked over at Ryan. He gave her his best effort at a friendly smile, but her face creased into an uncertain frown before she hustled back inside.

'Please, Mr Gasper,' Laura said, her own voice firming with each word. 'Meet me at the Upper Gum Tree Hotel at six tonight. We can talk there.'

And then she turned and walked away, leaving Ryan with little choice but to do as she asked.

Feeling Ryan Gasper's now staggeringly familiar gaze burning into her back, Laura picked up her washing basket, spun on her numb feet and hurried inside, the smile she had fashioned fast sliding into oblivion.

Will's brother had come, and he had her letter. No wonder she'd thought she had seen him somewhere before. He didn't look at all like Will, who had been barely nineteen, lean and lanky, with streaky blond hair when she had known him. But the something that had tugged at her subconscious was the fact that his deep, dark eyes were as vividly blue as her own daughter's.

In the intervening years since Will's funeral she had never heard back from his family, reasonably deducing that they either didn't believe her, wanted nothing to do with her, or simply didn't care. Truth be told, the more years that went by, the more that suited her just fine. But now here *he* was. The dashing, determined, older brother Will had yearned to equal, to emulate and, on the flipside, to disoblige as much as humanly possible. The brother who had not even deigned to show up at his funeral.

Laura shook her head to clear the returning fuzz. None of that mattered now. What mattered was that the time had come for Laura to share her darling little girl. He had said he wasn't there to cause her any trouble. Maybe. Maybe not. If he thought for a second that he could take Chloe away…

Laura's chest tightened as adrenalin kicked in. No matter how cool and self-assured Ryan Gasper's voice was, no matter how bewitching his gaze, how tempting his smile, or how Will had worshipped him, she didn't trust him as far as she could throw him. This was too important. The way she handled this, the way she handled him, would be *the* most important situation of her life.

'Mum!' Chloe called again. She bundled into the room, her strawberry-blonde ringlets pulled back into messy pigtails. 'Who was that man?'

'A friend,' Laura said, taking care how she approached the subject with Chloe. She instinctively chose not to create any sort of preconceived image of him. She had always taught Chloe to make up her own mind about people, not to listen to gossip.

She dumped the basket of wet clothes, with the dusty, dirty overalls splayed across the top, sat on the couch, tugged her daughter onto her lap, and held on tight. Too tight. Thankfully, Chloe didn't struggle away as she sometimes did when Laura became *mushy*.

'Now, what have you got there, possum?' Laura asked, her voice running on back-up power.

'I have to draw a picture of my family for school.' Chloe held out her crayon drawing of a house, a couple of animals, and a trio of people. 'I have you and me, Chimp and Irmela,' she said, referring to their pet fox terrier and overweight jersey cow respectively. 'And Jill is at the front gate. Is that enough?'

It always has been enough until now, Laura thought. 'I don't think you've missed anybody.'

'Well, Tammy is putting in all of her cousins. Even the ones who live in Scotland.' Chloe twisted on her lap to look her in the eye. 'Do I have any cousins in Scotland?'

Laura opened her mouth to say no, of course she didn't, but then she thought of the man in the black shiny car. Chloe might very easily have cousins all over the world, for all she knew.

From the moment Laura had posted her letter she had put the shoebox full of old clippings about Will under her bed, and had quite specifically *not* gone out of her way to hear about the Gasper family. But it seemed the time had come for her to peek at the world outside of her community, to find out about Chloe's extended family—and she had until six o'clock to figure out how to go about it.

Well, she had until six o'clock to finish the laundry, cook dinner, check Chloe's homework, finish the pies for the Country Women's Association meeting that night, *and* to figure out how she was going to handle the arrival of Ryan Gasper. The too hot bubble bath was so far down the list it dropped and fell away.

Once Chloe was ensconced back at the desk in her bedroom, Laura picked up the phone and dialled the Upper Gum Tree Hotel. When Jill answered the phone she all but blubbed with relief. 'Jill, it's Laura. We have a problem. I need you to set aside a table for me, and I need it to be discreet.'

CHAPTER TWO

THE UPPER GUM TREE HOTEL bustled with activity. Barflies lounged at the bar. Families conversed at a smattering of snug round dining tables. Local teenagers played snooker. And Ryan sat all on his lonesome in a secluded high-walled booth at the back of the room.

By the time six o'clock came and went he was onto his second beer and a young boy at the next table had taken a liking to him. The kid continued to stare over the top of the booth, and Ryan had no idea how to get rid of him.

He'd never had much experience dealing with kids. He had been nine years old when Will was born, and in boarding school by the time Will was three. By the time Ryan had left for university and beyond, they had spent little time together; Will, so quiet and shy, and intensely studious, had been practically a stranger to him. And to Jen's and Sam's kids he was merely cool Uncle Ryan, who brought presents whenever he came back from overseas.

But now he had another niece—a walking, talking remembrance of his little brother—and for some reason he felt an obligation to get to know this one properly. Half of him was energised by the prospect, and the other half wanted to wring Laura Somervale's pretty little neck for not trying harder to track his family down.

What reason could she possibly have for telling them about the little girl and then never contacting them again? It would have made more sense if she had never tried to contact them at all. It didn't add up, and as a guy who worked with checks and balances he planned to stick around at least until it did.

Perhaps she had simply found herself a new father for her daughter in the meantime. A strange sort of uncomfortable heat formed in Ryan's gut as he realised that she could even be married. Affianced. Living with someone. He hadn't counted on having to get through another man as well as Ms Somervale. He dearly hoped that he still wouldn't have to. Either way, if Laura Somervale didn't show in the next five minutes he was heading back out to the little weatherboard worker's cottage and he wasn't leaving until he had his answers.

Ryan gave in and crossed his eyes back at the kid who was still staring him down. He poked his tongue out and even added a humped back for good measure.

'So, did you find our Laura all right?' a female voice asked. Ryan uncrossed his eyes to find a short, round lady with boyish grey hair and bright button eyes leaning against the edge of the booth, beaming down at him. Jill Tucker. He had a feeling the woman knew exactly how he had found Laura, and what had transpired word for word.

'Yes, thanks,' he assured her with an unadorned smile. 'She was right where you told me she would be.'

'Of course she was,' she said, and her own smile grew larger. 'She's lived there since she was born. A dear girl, Laura. Would do anything to help any of us in a pickle, and if anyone ever dared to hurt her, or her little possum, they would have to deal with the rest of our town as well. Can I get you something to eat while you wait?'

Ryan blinked. It seemed Miss Somervale was not the only one who could so adeptly change tack mid-spiel.

Perhaps the idiosyncrasy could even be considered part of the local dialect.

'I'm happy with my beer,' he said. 'Thanks, anyway.'

Jill gave him a sympathetic smile before moving on to the next table. Before he even had the chance to take another sip, he was struck by the intoxicating scent of freshly baked apple pie. He had a famously sweet tooth, and the scent was so delicious he actually sniffed the air as a pair of cake boxes slid across his bench. In their wake came Laura Somervale. He was fairly sure it was her…

Gone were the messy curls, pulled back under a red bandana, and the graceful cotton dress had been replaced with an excessively frilly white shirt. She looked over her shoulder at the little boy peering over the next booth. 'Liam, your dessert is getting cold.'

The little boy disappeared from sight. Just like that. Wow. He would have to remember that trick. As she sat, Ryan opened his mouth to ask why she had gone to such trouble to dress in disguise, but when their eyes met he was rendered speechless yet again by the most startling difference from her earlier appearance. The sexiest dark smudges of eyeliner framed her pale brown eyes, making them glitter like gold. A searing flash of awareness overcame him. Had the flash come from him or from her?

'Sorry I'm late,' she said, her voice as crisp and curt with him as it had been with the little boy, Liam, and he figured any sort of responsiveness had been his alone. 'I had to get Chloe settled in at a friend's place first.'

So she hadn't left Chloe at home. She had sequestered her away somewhere unknown. No matter how promising her words, how valiant her smile, this woman was not as calm and trusting as she made out.

'So there's no one else at home who could have looked after her tonight? Your husband, perhaps?'

Laura coughed out a sorry laugh. 'Hardly,' she said, flapping a ring-free hand under his chin. 'Chloe and I are perfectly happy on our own.'

And, just like that, the uncomfortable lump in Ryan's mid-section faded away.

'Where are you staying?' she asked, shifting her weight on the soft leather seat.

'I have a room upstairs.'

'Nice?' she asked, still not looking him in the eye.

'Not sure. I haven't seen it yet. I came straight here from your place.'

'Oh, I just can't stand this,' she said suddenly, scrunching her eyes tight and banging her fists on the old wooden table.

Ryan's hands zoomed out to catch his glass of beer and stop it from overturning.

'I'm not bred for small talk,' she said, her voice earnest, her expression pleading. 'I'll be honest. Your being here scares the living daylights out of me.'

Ryan tried to disregard the divine scent of apples and sugar, and something else—an unexpectedly exotic perfume wafting from the direction of the woman in the equally exotic costume. 'You have no reason to fear me, Laura.'

'I have every reason!' She snapped her mouth shut, her fists closing tight atop the table. She seemed to collect herself, to temper her anguish. When she looked back at him from beneath her smoky lashes he knew she had found the calm in the eye of the storm.

'I had no brothers or sisters,' she continued, her voice now more controlled, though a tiny vibration gave her away. 'I have no aunts or cousins, distant or otherwise.

I understand that there are other people out there who are family to Chloe. You. You are her family. As such, you are the answer to her very dreams. And at least a very tiny, small but noisy part of me is relieved that you have finally come. But, at the same time, you also represent *my* very greatest fear. Losing her.'

Her anxious words brought about the image of tear stains on lavender paper, and he found it hard not to stare as he reconciled the heartfelt prose on that page with the plucky woman three feet from him now. Her honesty in that letter had amazed him, even while the news shocked him. Several years on, she was just as unwilling or unable to hold back her feelings as she had been then, and just as able to surprise him in person as she had been in print.

'I need to know your intentions,' she said. 'I can take it. I might not like it, but I can take it.'

His intentions? It was such an old-fashioned term but, coming from this wide-eyed country girl, it fitted. Though it made him feel like a rogue, he gave her the only truth he could. 'I don't exactly know.'

Her golden eyes glinted back at him in the low light. 'You're going to have to give me more than that if you think we can take this matter further.'

'What more do you want?'

'Proof that you are as nervous as I am.' She leaned forward, pinning him with her candid stare. 'I am an even mix of morbid embarrassment and stiff terror right now. When you wandered up onto my property, in your clean shirt and your new jeans, you must know I didn't for a second expect you to be…well, you. If you had, in fact, been a male stripper it would have shocked me less.'

'A male what?'

Laura bit her lip to stop herself from saying anything else she oughtn't. She filtered back through all the things she had mentally accused him of being, including an aluminium cladding salesman, but, no, the male stripper idea she had managed to keep to herself. Until now. She fluffed a hand over her face to try and divert him from her terminal case of foot-in-mouth disease.

She did want Chloe to meet her uncle. *Really* she did. For Chloe's sake how could she not? She was trying to think outside of her own selfish desire to keep her contented little existence intact because the big picture of Chloe's life meant so much more. Even though none of his superstar family had ever cared enough to write, to call, or to ask if Chloe was okay, she had to give him a chance. But, even so, there was a noisy little voice in her head that told her that *he* in particular was dangerous. Not cruel. Not insensitive to her fears. But somehow dangerous to her precariously balanced contentment. For a girl who felt as though a wonderful life was never quite within her grasp, she had no idea how to deal with a perpetual winner like the one seated before her.

'Stick to the subject, Mr Gasper. Why now? Why after all this time have you come?'

'*Your* letter brought me here, Ms Somervale.'

Her cheeks warmed as she thought of the words she had written in that letter. The words of a hormone-riddled, deeply sad, terrified, lonely and desperate teenager. But before she had a chance to ask to see the letter, which of course she would shovel into her mouth, chew and swallow so that no one else would ever know it existed, a shadow passed over the table. She looked up to find a man in dark trousers and a grey pullover smiling down at them.

'Hi, there, Father Grant,' she said, saving her request

for when they were alone again. She glanced over at Ryan and had no idea how to introduce him. Friend? Hardly. Chloe's uncle? She could barely believe it herself, much less say it aloud. Male stripper in the making? Now, that would probably cause less gossip in town than any of the other options on offer!

'Dress rehearsal tonight, Laura?' Father Grant asked.

Laura only then remembered her get-up. Oh, Lord! While Mr Perfect sat there looking so flawless, in his blue button-down shirt that did distracting things to his bluer than blue eyes, *she* was decked out in a mass of white frills and tight purple pants, with knee-high black boots jiggling skittishly below the table.

'Pirates of Penzance,' she blurted, for Ryan's benefit, flicking at a ruffle. 'The Country Women's Association is putting on the musical and I am playing the Pirate King.'

Ryan must have thought she was utterly insane, coming to meet him in such a get-up. And for singing to magpies. And for batting her eyelids at a stranger while all on her own out in an isolated Outback property... If he *were* intent on finding reasons to take her daughter away, he would surely have the beginnings of a list already.

'Isn't that a singing part?' Ryan asked.

Father Grant nodded. 'It is.'

Laura saw Father Grant shoot Ryan an ironic smile, and she all but harrumphed in response.

'The musical was all Laura's idea,' Father Grant continued. 'The local CWA are raising money for drought aid for local farmers who have been hit pretty hard over the last couple of years. Last year they did *Chicago*, and Laura's Matron Mama Morton brought down the house!'

'I'll bet it did,' Ryan said.

Laura didn't need to look at him to know that his face would be the picture of disbelief at Father Grant's kind words. She kept her head down as she picked at a flake of old paint on the tabletop.

'Our Laura is involved with numerous community projects,' Father Grant continued. 'She is President of the PTA and a volunteer firefighter, as well as infamous for undercharging for catering every event we throw in town. I don't know what we would do without her. Or little Chloe. They are family to all of us. We've just up and adopted them since Laura's dear father passed—haven't we, Laura?'

'Of course, Father Grant. You're the best.'

'Now, I'd better be off. Enjoy your meal.' He shot them a parting smile and Laura let out a shaky breath, thankful she had not had to introduce her companion.

'He seemed nice,' Ryan said. 'He certainly had a lot of good things to say about you.'

Laura brushed the praise away. 'Mr Gasper, if we keep beating around the bush like this I am likely to explode on the spot. Mr Gasper—'

'Call me Ryan, please.'

There was something in his voice, something low and intimate, that had her forgetting what she had been talking about in the first place. 'I just…' She took a moment to swallow. 'I know that this moment had to come. I only wonder why, seven years after the fact, that silly little letter of mine has sent you out looking for us.'

'I only just found your letter, Laura,' he explained. 'A couple of days ago. As the fates would have it, your letter never came to our attention at the time in which you sent it.'

Oh, God! Had they truly never known about her? About Chloe? She had never, not even once, thought that might be the reason why they had not come looking for her.

'I'm back in Australia for an extended stay for the first time in years,' he continued. 'At my family's request I have been cleaning up Will's effects. Seven years having passed since Will…died, no financial records need be kept any more. I discovered your letter unopened in amongst the great host of condolence letters.'

'Unopened?' Laura repeated, still coming to terms with Ryan's bombshell.

'At the time, my family received so many condolence letters—from friends, acquaintances, readers of my sister's magazine, fans of my parents' documentary films, even many of your neighbours. My family read as many as they could, but after a couple of weeks found they couldn't keep up. It was too much. Too hard. In the end they posted a half-page thank-you note in the *Australian* newspaper to all who had Will in their thoughts.'

Laura noticed Ryan's dulcet voice was unnaturally even. Though he held eye contact with her the whole time, the poor man was struggling just as she was with the situation. Nevertheless, she fought back the desire to take his fisted hand in hers, to unpeel his tightly clenched fingers and rub some warmth back into them.

'Mum and Dad went back to Brunei to finish the film they were working on,' he said. 'Jen was already back on a musical tour of the United States. And Sam had just had her second child and couldn't cope with the task. All of Will's correspondence was forwarded to our family accountant, who kept on track with bills and tax correspondence, and simply filed everything else. When cleaning out the files this week I found one folder with several unopened letters. Including yours.'

Laura realised he hadn't included himself in the list

of people available to read the letters and look after the formalities. Where *had* he been when his family had needed him? she wondered. Why hadn't he been at the funeral? But she heard the steady thread of regret in his voice that he was trying so hard to mask. So she let it go. 'And...and your family?' she asked, when she found her voice again. 'Your sisters and parents? Do they know about me?'

'Only Sam. She was with me when I found your letter, and would have come too if not for having three kids under ten herself. As to the others, no. Not yet. We thought it better to find out if you had—'

He stopped, and for the first time was discomfited enough to look away.

'If I had gone through with the pregnancy?' she finished for him, biting down the bitter taste the very thought brought. But it wasn't his fault. He was only being honest. 'And now that you know that I did?'

He looked back at her, the deep, steady blue gaze creating patches of warmth on her skin wherever it touched.

'Well, now I think it would be best for Chloe to get used to me first,' he said, 'before the whole Gasper gang descends upon her. We can be formidable as a united front.'

A tiny portion of the tension in Laura's shoulders eased. Surely, if that was his ultimate plan, he would have brought the might of the Gasper clan down on her with a vengeance? It seemed there was a streak of compassion within the self-assured outer shell.

The bell over the door jingled as a group of chattering women in pirate garb jumbled into the restaurant. Their beady, kohl-smudged eyes searched the restaurant.

Ryan felt the chance to get to his own questions slipping away. Somehow, with her smoky eyes and bold honesty, her bare feet and knee-high boots, her glossy curls and red bandana, she had managed again and again to keep the conversation as one-sided as she pleased. She had found out his side of the story and he still knew nothing of hers. He wondered if it was entirely accidental, or whether, despite all her *I really want you to meet Chloe* promises, she would be happier if that never eventuated at all.

'That lot are looking for me,' Laura said. 'I'm sorry to leave this hanging mid-air, but I do have to go.'

She stood, and he grabbed her hand. 'So when do I get to meet her?' he asked.

Laura stared at their entwined fingers for a few moments before her glittery golden eyes swung to face him, her head cocked to one side.

'Chloe,' he clarified. 'When do I get to meet her properly? I hoped that was what this secret meeting was all about.'

'Half the town is at this restaurant, Mr Gasper,' she said. 'This meeting is hardly a secret.' He knew then that she was wilfully misunderstanding him. Her obstructiveness was no accident. Behind the pretty eyes, this woman's mind had not stopped ticking all night.

If he could figure a way through her labyrinthine thinking, maybe he would end up on her side rather than three steps behind. At least now he knew what made the Upper Gum Tree Hotel at six o'clock on a Sunday night so special. She'd figured that if he was going to make demands, she would have *half the town* as witnesses.

'Well, obviously my presence here is not a secret. Why else would I have had people lining up to give you glowing testimonials?'

She made to protest, then seemed to realise what

Father Grant's speech had been about. So that at least hadn't been her doing. A soft blush crept across her cheeks—a pretty blush, seriously becoming, distracting enough for him to forget what he was accusing her of in the first place. 'That had nothing to with me,' she said, giving his hand a light tug. 'Though I have some idea who to blame.'

Realising her hand was still in his, he let go, the feel of smooth skin slipping across his palm momentarily unsettling. *Enough!* he scolded himself. He stood, determined to get them back on an even footing.

'It's a meeting secreted away from the one person for whom the meeting is most important,' he said, his voice stern and implacable. 'Make a time. Set a date. Now. Or I may decide not to believe all your promises that you do want me to meet Chloe. How about tomorrow morning?'

She blinked, and he saw the moment her ticking mind switched into overdrive. 'Tomorrow is Monday. She has school.'

'What about after school?'

'Pony club. Then violin practice.'

Violin. Just like Jen. She had known he was an economist. Did she know about Jen, too? Could that have prompted the choice of instrument? The thought warmed him more than he thought sensible. 'And dinner time?' he asked, determined not to let her sway the conversation again.

'She has homework. And her bedtime is eight o'clock.'

She was relentless. He bit back a smile.

'Soon,' she promised, obviously realising as much herself. 'But on my terms. She's a cluey kid, outrageously bright, and even more sensitive for it. We need to tread carefully.'

He nodded. She could have been describing Will at Chloe's age. 'So when?'

The twittering sound of pirate-garbed women grew louder behind him, and when Laura all but melted with relief he knew he was too late. 'Saved by your merry men,' he said under his breath, and she had the good grace to blush even more.

'Laura!' one of the women called out. 'If you're not ready to rehearse we could grab a quick shandy?'

'No, no, no. I'm done here,' Laura said, moving into the protective haven of the colourful group.

'Laura is such a darling,' one of the ladies said out of the blue. 'I can't read so well any more, so she always helps me with my lines.'

Ryan had a feeling she had been *helped* with her current lines as well. 'Does she, now?' he asked, unable to stop the smile tugging at his mouth.

'I was overseas last spring when my daughter fell ill,' another said, after getting a nudge in the ribs. 'And, even though spring is the worst time for Chloe and her asthma, she and Laura made the long trip via my daughter's house every day to get her little ones to school.'

Ryan could tell Laura wanted to slap a hand across each of their mouths, but she just stood back and let them vent. It reminded him of a passage from one of Will's e-mails to Sam, which she had shared with him when they were going through Will's papers:

The people here are amazing, Sam. Kind, generous, selfless, opinionated, and meddlesome! You can't scratch your nose without somebody knowing about it. And you can be sure that within the day everyone in town will know about it too. I thought it might be infuriating, but it's not. It means that there are people who care about you. So, no matter how far away we all actually live from one another, we know that we are never really alone.

It seemed that Will had been right on the money. The town knew exactly who *he* was, and had turned up in force to make sure he knew exactly who Laura was too.

'Our Laura is an angel,' the ringleader said.

'Esme, seriously, that's enough,' Laura murmured.

'From what I have heard tonight,' Ryan butted in, 'I would say sainthood is not far away.'

The ladies all grinned back at him, knowing they had all successfully played their parts in the night's hastily organised small play.

'Will you be coming to see the musical?' Esme asked.

'You never know your luck,' he responded with a wink, and with that the three grey-haired pirates left in a twitter, and he and Laura were again left alone in the room full of people.

'So,' he said.

'So,' she returned. 'I'd better go after them. If I'm not there within a minute they'll be back for shandies. And their husbands will all be onto me first thing in the morning complaining that the play is just a front for the Country Women's *Drinking* Association.'

She reached over and grabbed her cooling apple pies, turned and walked away. It seemed their meeting was over.

'Isn't the Pirate King a male part as well as a singing part?' he called out curiously, not yet wanting the encounter to end.

Laura spun on her knee-high black boots but kept

walking away from him. 'Not so many males in the Country Women's Association,' she explained.

'Isn't that discriminatory?'

'So join!' she said, throwing out her hands. 'Be my guest. You can even take my part.' She tore off the bandana and a mass of auburn curls spilled onto her shoulders. She fluttered the bandana towards him, and when he didn't accept the offer she spun about and walked away.

'I'll see *you* tomorrow,' Ryan warned.

'I don't doubt it,' she called, as she waved the bandana over her shoulder and headed out of a side door, slamming it behind her.

Ryan stood staring into space. The image of those tight purple pants would take some time to dissolve from his memory. But all he had was time. For the first time in…for ever he had nothing planned: no jobs lined up, no reports to complete, only the final edits on the textbook with the complementary CD to turn in to his editor.

He slid back into the booth and nursed his now warm beer. Chatter and laughter from the other patrons filtered back into his awareness. And he was left…wanting.

The last sentence of Will's e-mail to Sam came back to him.

> *…no matter how far away we all actually live from one another, we know that we are never really alone.*

Had his brother really felt so alone in the great hustle and bustle of Melbourne? Had he needed his scattered family around him that much? And had living around these people really made all the difference?

Ryan remembered the last time he and Will had spoken, and tried to see if he had missed the signs of Will's isolation even then…

Ryan's hotel room phone rang. He was on his way to a black-tie function in the piazza in front of the Pantheon in Rome. He thought about not answering, but a quick glance at his watch showed he had time.

'Ryan Gasper,' he answered.

'This is a collect call from Tandarah, Australia,' the operator said in English, with a strong Italian accent.

'I'll accept,' Ryan said, slumping down onto the side of his bed. 'Will, is that you?'

'Yeah.' His little brother breathed out.

'Excellent. So, are you coming? I'm off to Paris in three days, so I can just meet you there. My PA back in Melbourne is ready to book everything the second you say yes.'

'Well, actually, bro,' Will said, his voice so heavy and glum Ryan pretty much knew what was coming before he even spoke, 'that's what I was calling about. I'm not coming.'

Ryan rubbed his hand across suddenly tight eyes. 'You can't possibly tell me you've had a better offer.'

'Actually, I have.'

For the briefest of moments Ryan's heart skipped a beat. 'You've taken the scholarship offer at Oxford?'

'Umm, no. You see, there's this girl…'

Ryan leapt off the bed and strode back and forth across the room, as far as the telephone cord would allow. 'Will, do we have to have this conversation again? You don't know how good you have it, kid. I don't know how many more times any of us can stick our necks out for you. You can't keep turning away the opportunities we have created for you.'

'But, bro, this is an opportunity I have created for myself.'

'Considering who you are, I would hazard a guess she is the opportunist in this scenario.'

'That's way harsh, bro, and so far off the mark it's funny. Maybe you should give up the Paris thing and come visit me instead. Meet her. See this place. It's phenomenal.'

'Be serious.'

Will's exasperation broke through. 'God, you just don't get it, do you? I can never be you! Out here I feel like I don't have to be, either. I can be somebody new. Somebody I like.'

The red light on Ryan's phone began to flash. His taxi was waiting downstairs. 'Look, Will, I have to go. Just tell me you're still considering Paris, okay?'

A deep heartfelt sigh wafted down the phone line. 'Sure,' Will said. 'Okay.'

'I'll talk to you again in a couple of days, and by that time I hope to hear better news. Take care.'

Ryan hung up the phone, his whole body thrumming with frustration. It hurt so much that the kid was letting this time slip through his fingers. The last thing he wanted was for his little brother to look back on his wasted youth with regret. He should have been studying, travelling, networking, embracing the world—not some hick chick in the middle of the Outback.

He picked up his keys, slipped his wallet into the hidden pocket in his tuxedo jacket and left. Next week. Next week when he was in Paris he would call him back and try to talk some more sense into the kid.

Of course by that stage Will would probably be done with the whole farming dream. He would have become bored with the girl and decided to become a fire-stick twirler in Byron Bay.

Tremendous…

Coming back to the present, Ryan caught Jill's eye at the bar and she came straight over.

'Another beer?' she asked.

He shook his head. 'But there is something else you can do for me.'

She raised an eyebrow and waited.

'Who is the local real-estate agent?'

'That would be Cal Bunton.'

'Let's get Cal Bunton on the phone, then, shall we? Let him know I have some business I need to conduct. It has to be tonight, but I will make it worth his while.'

CHAPTER THREE

THE next morning Ryan knew better than to park his car beneath the flowering banksia in front of Kardinyarr House. The day before it had dropped spiky red petals all over the roof of his car, leaving a horrible sticky residue it had taken him a half-hour to clean away.

He parked his car beside the house, got out, and, stretching his arms over his head, walked the last few metres to the edge of the yard, until he could see over the rise to the gully at the rear of the property.

Kardinyarr: two-hundred hilly acres of grazing land that had grabbed his brother so tight he had been willing to give up a very different sort of life for it. And for her.

Clouds brushed large patches of shadow across the huge, dusty green parcel of land. Ghost gums collected in majestic pockets on the hilltops. Hardy lantana and sturdy low-lying scrub wound in a curling thick mass alongside a meandering creek in the gully below. It was so quiet he could hear leaves skittering across the roof of the house, the windows creaking against the buffeting breeze. What he could *not* hear was traffic, or televisions, or barking dogs.

It *was* picturesque, just as Will had described in his e-mails to Sam, just as he had tried to tell Ryan on the telephone that night in Rome. But Ryan needed more. He wanted to understand. Needed to understand. Because it seemed that until he could reconcile Will's decision to stay, he couldn't let him off the hook, couldn't let him go.

Ryan headed back to the car and pulled a couple of bags of groceries from the passenger seat just as Laura drove up the driveway in her old grey hatchback. She skidded to a halt at an angle in the middle of a patch of grass, leapt from the car, and stormed towards him. Today's cotton sundress was white with ripe cherries. Today's ponytail was tied back with a proper red ribbon. Today she wore flat white sandals that kicked up clouds of dust as she raged over to him.

'What? No purple pants?' he asked.

She ignored him, just as he'd expected her to. 'I just ran into Cal Bunton, dropping his daughter off at Chloe's school, and he told me what you've done.'

And there he'd been, wondering how he would tell Laura the good news, when he should have guessed she would know before the ink had even dried on the contracts. He hitched the grocery bags onto his hip, shut his car door, pressed the remote lock, reminded himself he really didn't need to do that any more, and then headed towards the house.

'I have been pleasant,' Laura raved, stamping along behind him. 'Heck, I haven't made nearly as much of a fuss at your landing on my doorstep without any warning as I could have. Now you have gone and *bought* Kardinyarr and you're moving in? Just like that?'

'Well, not quite just like that,' Ryan said, balancing the groceries precariously as he reached into his jeans pocket for the front door keys. 'A quick settlement suits both buyer and seller, so Kardinyarr should be mine within the fortnight. Until then I'm leasing the place from the Callaghans.'

'But how could you?'

'It seems that I had to. I will have a good chance of actually *meeting* your daughter this way. Unless, of course, she'll be at school, or slumber parties, or busy with super-important first grade homework for evermore.'

Laura blithely ignored his sideways barb. 'Cal Bunton also said you were asking his advice on running livestock. Are you seriously thinking of working this place?'

Nice move, he thought. *If you can't win the argument, change the subject.* 'I seriously am.'

'But what do you know about running a farm?'

Without looking over his shoulder, he opened the door and headed inside his empty house. 'I know a lot about agriculture. In fact, the paper I was brought to Australia to present focused on the importance of the cotton industry in South East Queensland to the Australian economy. Nothing like harnessing the best natural resources the world has to offer to keep our economy chugging along nicely.'

Only once he'd reached the kitchen and placed the groceries on the empty bench did he realise she hadn't followed. He poked his head into the hall to find her fuming out on the grass. He threw his keys onto the bench and walked back to the doorway.

She threw her arms out in frustration. 'Well, so long as you can learn what you need to know from a chat with a bunch of cronies around a conference table, you're laughing!'

'I'm also about halfway through reading *Running Livestock for Dummies*, and I am finding the cartoons and pie charts most helpful.'

She blinked, obviously trying to decide if he was, in fact, serious. She started to shuffle from one foot to the other, scrunching her once neat and tidy dress into tight fists.

'But I would be happy to take any advice you wish

to impart,' he said, knowing it would get her goat even more.

'Oh, rack off,' she blurted.

And he laughed. Really laughed. She looked so sweet, all dolled up in her enticing little outfit, but beneath the pretty face and the county-girl candour she was as spicy as they came. 'I have never met an adult so hyperactive,' he said. 'Can I recommend Vitamin B1?'

She crossed her arms and he knew she couldn't calm herself even if she wanted to. 'While we are sharing *advice*, Kardinyarr is *no* place for a hobby farm!'

'I have no intention of setting up a *hobby farm*, Laura. I don't believe in doing anything halfway. Never have. All or nothing is the only way to live. I have a feeling you share that sentiment.'

'Well, that's just fine and dandy,' she said, her voice suddenly eerily calm. 'But I should warn you we've had city gents come out this way before, and they *never* last past six months.'

Will. The name slammed into Ryan's thoughts, and he saw the second it slammed into Laura's as well. Will had not lasted *two* months before the harsh reality of life at Kardinyarr had killed him. A brown snake. His clever brother, with his whole future out there, just waiting for him to grab a hold, had died from a tiny little snake bite. Laura's mouth dropped open, her whole face fell, and he felt the apology as surely as if she had said it aloud.

'Just come inside, Laura. I make no promises about being here six months from now, but until then I'll still need to find a home for all my groceries, and I'm sure you would just love to tell me where to put them.'

Her mouth snapped shut, her contrition warring with her fighting spirit. Then her gaze flickered and rambled down his form, taking in his clean fingernails, his pressed jeans, his shiny boots. When it slithered back up to meet his eye, he knew… Her spirit had won.

'I'm sorry, *Cowboy*,' she said, her voice lingering on the final word, 'but I don't think you could last six *weeks* before the bright lights of the big city called you home.'

'Clothes do not maketh the man, *sweetheart*.'

She grew red in the face as he returned with his own endearment. 'Then why not just stick to a suit and tie? Unless you're trying to convince people otherwise.'

Touché. Oh, she was good at this. But he wasn't done yet. 'Haven't you heard the phrase, "Dress for the job you want, not the job you have"?' *Gotcha!*

That was enough to have her huffing off back to her car and careering up the driveway to her own house. He would have liked to follow, if only to know what she was accusing him of this time, but another car had just pulled in behind his. It was a dusty van with 'Tandarah Antiques' written in scrawling ye olde script on the side.

'Mr Gasper?' the driver said as he hauled his heavy bulk from the front seat of the van. The name 'Bill' was stitched into his shirt.

'That's me—Bill.' Ryan shook the big man's sweaty hand, and gave a short nod to his cohort in the passenger seat.

'So, where do you want the credenza?'

'I'm sorry. The what?'

'The credenza.'

'Nope. I still have no idea what you are saying, mate. You'll have to try translating that into *male speak*.'

'A great hunk of wood in which you keep the family china.' The delivery guy looked down at his folder. 'Kardinyarr House. For R. Gasper from S. Gasper-Jackson.'

Aah. He had called his sister Sam the night before, to

update her about young Chloe and to let her know his plans for Kardinyarr and obstinate Laura Somervale. She had insisted on sending him a housewarming gift purchased from a store in Tandarah. Something with a *country flavour*, she had promised, as though living in a sprawling home on two hundred acres wasn't *country* flavoured enough. But it was good of her, nonetheless. A token gift to show she understood his sabbatical and approved.

'Oh. The *credenza*. Umm, in the dining room?' He wished he had paid more attention to the multitude of home renovation shows on TV. But Bill seemed satisfied by his response, so he must have subconsciously picked something up along the way.

Ryan was momentarily distracted by a flicker of lace curtain from inside the cottage next door. He had asked Sam to hold off telling his parents and their sister Jen about Chloe. And Laura. His family were overwhelming enough in grander circles much less in a quiet haven such as this. But they would come. They were just those sort of people. Tolerant. Understanding. Adaptable. In that regard, *he* was the Gasper born of a different mould. He liked things the way he liked them. He didn't know if he had it in him to compromise, though Laura Somervale was certainly out to make him try.

He looked over to the cottage again. Yep. Definite curtain-flicking going on over there. With a small smile, Ryan followed the hulking great credenza-whatsit into his new home.

Mortified that she had been caught staring, Laura stormed into her kitchen, looking to lose herself there.

As a teenager, living alone with her dad, she had learned early on that if she wanted to eat anything more exciting than scrambled eggs she would have to cook it for herself. She had soon found the kitchen was a place in which she could daydream, where she could whisk away her gravest demons and cook up her most sublime fantasies. At that moment she felt a great desire to beat the heck out of something.

Within fifteen minutes of unmeasured pouring, gratifying egg-cracking and manic batter-whipping, she had a chocolate cake baking in the oven. The bulk of her vexation exhausted out of her, she leant against the kitchen bench and stared out of the window. She looked down the length of her slim five-acre block, past the undulating paddock with its fallen trees—home to a new family of rabbits—past a line of fruit trees which would be ripe for the picking any day now, past the low-lying dam where Chloe's plump pet cow, Irmela, was taking a drink beneath the shade of a tree, and out into nothingness.

It seemed Ryan Gasper was not going to be hoodwinked into vanishing out of her life. Soon she would have to sit Chloe down and have *the* conversation she had been preparing herself for since the day her little possum was born.

Laura's ribs suddenly felt too tight in her chest. With a hearty sniff, she headed to the bedroom to change. She stopped when she caught sight of herself in the mirror at the end of the hall. Her hair was falling from its constraint. Her dress was crushed and a patch of cocoa stained one hip. Darn it! It was one of her nice dresses.

She had only been popping out to drop Chloe at school, but she had dressed up in more than her usual old jeans, T-shirt and flip-flops. Why? In case she bumped into *him*, that was why. She had to look good for him. She had to look like a good mother. His family had power. Influence. She had a fair idea that if they wanted to whip Chloe away from her they would know the right person to talk to.

She leaned forward and pinched some colour into her cheeks. 'Argh!' she growled at her reflection. 'Of course you did not dress up to look like a good mother. You are a single mother, wasting away on a hill top, miles from the nearest anybody, and one smile from some hot city boy sends you to the far reaches of your closet in search of something girly to wear. You are pathetic!'

Then she remembered she was no longer miles from anybody. For the first time in several years she had a neighbour. And not just any neighbour, not just any hot city boy, but Ryan Gasper.

Though she didn't want Chloe to have a preconceived idea of the man, Laura didn't have that luxury. During her short time with Will she and he had talked and talked and talked. Whereas most of Laura's talks had been about how she felt about losing her father, most of Will's talks had concerned his relationship with his all-too-successful big brother. Through Will's eyes she had come to imagine Ryan as whip-smart, confident, and larger than life. Everything that at that time she wasn't. So much so that even now his name still brought about a chemical reaction inside of her.

'Add opinionated, irritating, and utterly frustrating!' she yelled into the mirror.

She undid the zip of her dress with more effort than necessary, whipped the dress over her head, threw it at the dirty-clothes basket in her room, grabbed her faded old jeans and her oldest, plainest T-shirt, and dressed herself back as Laura Somervale, farmer's daughter.

And if anybody had a problem with that, they could take it up with her!

* * *

A knock sounded at Ryan's front door. He put away the last of his dry groceries, wiped flour dust from his palms and approached the front door, feeling more invigorated than he ought to at the thought of sparring with Ms Somervale yet again. He opened the door, but it wasn't Laura.

'Morning, Jill,' he said, and even he heard the regret in his voice. *Badly done, Ryan.*

'Were you expecting somebody else?' Her sharp gaze shot across the way to the small cottage next door, to the house with the fluttering curtains.

'Not at all. Especially considering nobody bar you, Cal Bunton, the previous owners and my sister have been told I'll be staying here.'

She reached out and slapped his face softly. 'You are a dear boy for even pretending to think that would be the case. Now, invite me in. I come bearing fruit!'

She pulled back a teatowel covering the basket in her arms to reveal an abundance of banana muffins.

'Come on in.' He stood back to let her pass. 'You have beaten my furniture here, so I can't offer you a seat. All I can offer is a viewing of what I'm told is a credenza.'

'Lead the way.'

He did as he was told, escorting Jill into the dining room where she stared at the sideboard with wide eyes.

'Now, that's impressive!' she exclaimed.

Ryan stood beside her and crossed his arms. 'It really is, isn't it? Somebody cut down a forest to build that thing.'

'Mmm. I'm glad to see the place filling up with life again, Ryan. I'll bet Laura will be just as thrilled to have somebody living here after all these years.'

Ryan knew he could have won a lot of money taking that bet. 'You think so, do you, Jill?'

'Sure. She loves this place like nobody else.' She fluttered a hand around the all but empty space before it sank to her side.

Ryan had a sudden feeling he was being railroaded. He felt a big empty pit open up inside of him and almost didn't want to ask. 'And why is that?'

'Lady Laura has looked after the upkeep on this place for years, knowing the overseas owners didn't give a hoot. It was nothing more than a nest egg for them. But for her? So many memories. For years she's kept Kardinyarr up to nick, even organising tradesmen to look it over each spring. We always kind of hoped she would win the Lotto, so she could make an offer on the place.'

Now the song-and-dance act made even more sense. He was turning into Laura's every nightmare rolled into one.

'She is the jewel of the region and she has lain dormant for all too long. So if you don't do right by her, the whole town will lynch you for sure,' Jill said, with a huge grin spread across her face.

Ryan wasn't so sure if Jill was now talking about Kardinyarr, or the lady who had kept it looking rosy for so many years. He decided to take Jill's words at face value. 'I have no plans to tear the place down, Jill, or subdivide, or deck it out in modern furniture. I'm sure you can pass that on to the good folks of Tandarah for me.'

'Excellent. I'll quote you on the specials board at the Upper Gum Tree.'

Ryan laughed, but he had a feeling that Jill had it in her to follow through.

'You weren't kidding, were you?' she said, wandering

through the rest of the house, spying the fact that he didn't have a fridge or a microwave. All he had in the kitchen was an old kettle. On the floor of the lounge room he had laid out a comforter, pillow, and sheets borrowed from Jill's hotel, and an overnight bag, which he'd had with him when he first arrived.

'But who needs a table, right?' Jill said. 'Out here we make do. Follow me.'

Jill led him out to the back veranda, where they sat, legs dangling over the edge, and shared the still warm muffins. He wasn't doing anything much—he wasn't making plans, or forging budgets, or negotiating agreements—but he was enjoying himself immensely. This wasn't a bad way to spend a morning.

'Did you grow these yourself?' he asked through a mouthful of banana muffin.

Jill's grin returned. 'Don't tell anyone, but it's a packet mix! Laura is the chef in the region. Give her a bite of any dessert and she can reproduce it blindfolded. So, as I figure it, there's no reason in competing.'

'I love your reasoning. And I like your muffins—home-grown or not.'

'And I like you, Ryan Gasper, though I probably should not. Considering who you are, on so many levels, I am sure I ought to be extremely wary of you.'

She looked over at him with a gaze so intense Ryan knew lesser mortals would quite easily crumble to sand at her feet. 'Promise me you are not going to be a fly-by-night farmer. That would be too sad. Not nearly enough dashing young economists with cheeky glints in their eyes around these parts.'

'I know of at least one person who thinks there is one too many of me in town already.'

Jill gave him a squeeze on the shoulder. 'Nevertheless,

she will do her best to broker a peaceful accord between you for Chloe's sake—because she's too kind for the likes of you and me.'

Jill dragged herself to her feet with a great heaving sigh. 'Take advantage of that goodness and there are a million places I could bury you out here and you would never be found. Keep the muffin basket. If you're here long enough to see me again, you can give it to me then.'

Then she was gone. Off the veranda and around the side of the house before Ryan had a chance to disassemble her words.

He uncurled his lanky frame from the edge of the veranda and rounded the house in time to see Jill take off in her rusty, once-white ute. She crunched the gears and drove down the long sloping driveway in a swirl of dust.

It seemed the people of Tandarah had nothing but good to say about Laura Somervale. And they went out of their way to say it too. Ryan wondered if his own friends would go to the same lengths to say they believed in him. Since all of his friends lived thousands of miles from one another, in cities all around the world, the best he would ever hope for would be the odd dissolute telegram.

But what did he expect? He had been deliberately gung-ho and adventurous all his life. Taking advantage of every opportunity. Travelling wherever the dollar and the city lights shone brightest. That didn't leave much room for putting down roots.

And perhaps he had not been the most supportive brother Will could have wished for. Jeez, even after Will had died he had kept working. Ryan rubbed a rough hand over his face, massaging his eyes as he imagined the remainder of his family, huddled against the cold on that windy, wet, Melbourne winter's day…

Ryan sat in the window of his hotel room in Paris, staring through the drizzly sky over the grey rooftops to the tip of Notre Dame's spiralling spires, hazy in the distance.

When he blinked, his focus shifted. The grey raindrops trickling down the windowpane made it look as though he was crying. But on that day no tears came.

On that day, ten thousand miles away, on the other side of the world, in a small private cemetery in Melbourne, Australia, his younger brother was being buried. Ryan didn't feel tears. He felt utterly at a loss.

Will had been such a smart kid. A student with immense aptitude. A kid with a scholarship to study commerce law at Oxford. But a kid who, without blinking, had turned it down. Will had had no goals. No gumption. He never had.

Being several years older, and a heck of a lot more streetwise, Ryan had done his best over the years to guide him, to offer advice, even to use his own political influence to get Will interviews, to get him noticed, to get him on track.

He had, even as recently as a week earlier, offered to buy Will a ticket to Paris—a ticket to join him at the World Economic Summit where he was set to give the keynote speech. He had hoped that his success, a glimpse of his own energetic lifestyle, would inspire his brother to grab hold of the opportunities life had afforded him and not look back.

But, no. Will had preferred to live like a hippy in some Outback town and he had been happy to stay there, living off his Christmas money for ever if he could manage it. All for the sake of some girl. Some farm girl he'd just met.

Ryan had revelled in the intensity of his frustration. He'd wanted to take Will by the scruff of the neck and shake some sense into him. But now it was too late. Will was gone. Dead. All that latent talent wasted. All that wonderful, fruitful, eminent Gasper blood spilled into the earth.

Frustrated to the point of fury, Ryan lashed out a punch at the drizzly windowpane, and the glass cracked and smashed. He didn't even feel the pain, didn't even know he had injured himself until the first blood-red drop landed upon his pale grey suit pants…

Ryan stretched out his hand, staring at the long scar across his knuckles. He had refused stitches at the time, preferring to bandage the wound himself. It hadn't healed as well as it could have, and he could still feel it sting on cold days.

Ryan looked over at the cottage next door, the flickering curtains now still. Maybe now was the time to put past mistakes behind him. With this new project, this new house, this new family member, maybe he had been given the chance to prove that when it came to the crunch, a 'fly-by-night' tendency wasn't his defining characteristic.

CHAPTER FOUR

LATE Monday afternoon Ryan had still heard no word about the rest of his furniture, which Sam had organised to send up from his apartment in Melbourne, but he did receive a phone call to say Betsy had arrived. He hadn't seen her in a couple of months and, so, rather than his usual one-off visit every few weeks, he had some real time to spend with her.

Marking his place in his book—which was *not*, in fact, *Running Livestock for Dummies*, but close enough that he did not need Ms Somervale catching him reading it—Ryan grabbed his keys and headed out. Jogging down the front steps, he pulled up short when he found a visitor in floral jeans, pink sneakers and a *Little Mermaid* T-shirt playing jump rope in front of his house. His breath hitched as a pair of cool blue Gasper eyes looked back at him. *Chloe.*

He looked up at the cottage next door but saw no sign of Laura. 'You must be Chloe,' he said.

The little girl spun around as she skipped. 'And you must be Mr Gasper.'

Ryan shot a glance towards the quiet cottage. 'Did your mother tell you who I was?' he asked, feeling a mite sneaky but more than a mite interested in her answer.

She nodded, skipping-rope thumping rhythmically against the dirt. 'Mum said that you come from the city, and that you will be living in Kardinyarr House for now.'

Huh. Unless the little girl was editing her mother's words, it seemed that Laura Somervale was above spreading her *spicy* feelings towards him to her daughter.

'And before she told me to go play with my skip rope,' Chloe continued, 'I heard her on the phone, telling Auntie Jill that even though you fill out a pair of blue jeans just fine, that doesn't make you a real farmer.'

Ryan bit back a laugh. So, smart-mouthed Laura Somervale liked the way he filled out his jeans. Ryan felt himself grow at least an inch taller at the notion.

'What did my Mum tell you about *me*?' Chloe asked.

Ryan paused, suddenly finding himself on rocky ground again. 'She did say that you are a heck of a horsewoman.'

'I won a blue ribbon a couple of weeks ago.'

Ryan imagined her sitting atop a pony, blue ribbon pinned to her chest. He wished he had been around to see that, to see the smile spread across that earnest little face. 'Well, Chloe, now we know so much about each other, I think it would be all right if you called me Ryan.'

She nodded again, and this time there was even a hint of a smile, with a sweet dimple on her right cheek. 'Good, because I would laugh if I had to say Gasper all the time.'

His own smile slipped. 'Why would that make you laugh?'

'Because Gasper is my middle name.'

Well, Laura Somervale certainly hadn't told him that.

'Gasper was my dad's last name,' Chloe continued. 'He lived in your house before I was born. He came from the city, too.'

Ryan had no idea how to broach the minefield of statements that Chloe had so innocently blurted out.

Again he looked to the cottage, but there was no hint that Laura was aware the two of them were chatting. He suddenly wished for some curtain-flickering, or some atrocious singing by the clothesline.

Then Chloe came out with a jaw-dropper. 'My friend Tammy says that her mum said that you're my uncle.'

'Whoa!' What to say? If Laura thought he had overstepped the boundaries she would surely snap him in two. This would take some fancy dancing. 'Did you…? Have you talked to your mum about that?'

Chloe shook her head. 'I forgot until now.'

'Well, how about you and your Mum have a longer chat about me when she gets off the phone.'

'They're chatting about something I'm not allowed to listen to so she sent me outside. I told her I'm old enough to know everything.'

'Mums are usually pretty good at knowing when little girls are ready to know everything.'

'I guess.' Then, after barely a pause, she asked, 'Do I have any cousins in Scotland? My friend Tammy has cousins in Scotland. Mum says Scotland is cold and green, and that the men wear skirts. I've never seen a man wear a skirt. Do you wear skirts?'

Yep. Definitely Laura Somervale's daughter, he thought, marvelling at Chloe's fluctuating speech pattern. At first he had found it too fast to follow; now he found it downright endearing. Not wanting to fall prey to her conversational trickery, he reached out, scuffed her hair, and said, 'You never know your luck. Now, maybe you should check if your mum is off the phone.'

Chloe shrugged mid-skip. Ryan was surprised to find he was genuinely loath to leave her sight, but he had pushed his luck long enough. 'It was nice to finally meet you, Chloe *Gasper* Somervale. I hope we can chat again soon.' With that, he turned and jogged towards his car.

'Where are you going?' Chloe asked, her rope not stopping as she skipped alongside him.

'I'm going flying,' Ryan said.

That stopped her short. Her skipping-rope slumped at her pink sneakers and her head tipped to one side as she looked at him as if he was making up stories. All serious and untrusting. All Somervale.

He crouched down until he was at eye level with her. 'You know the airstrip out back of the Mackay place?'

Chloe nodded.

'Well, I have my very own plane parked over there right now. Her name is Betsy, and I'm more excited than a kid at a funfair about seeing her again.'

Her hands shot to her hips. 'You have no such thing!' she said, and again she looked so like her mother.

'Have you ever been in a plane?' he asked.

'Once. Jill drove us into Melbourne, which took two hours, then we flew to Sydney to meet a doctor for my asthma, and that took an hour. We were home again the same day. He gave me a new puffer that tastes the worst.'

'Well, my plane isn't a big white jumbo, like that plane, it's more like the size of a truck. It's a Cessna Skyhawk 172R, an all-metal, single-engine piston, high-wing monoplane with a four-person seating capacity.'

Chloe blinked at him. 'Our plane was red.'

And then he remembered. He wasn't making conversation with some political flunky at a cocktail party—he was speaking to a six-year-old. It seemed that Ryan hadn't developed a way to communicate with people that much younger than himself overnight, after all.

'You went in a red plane? Now, *that* is impressive.

Red planes are always the fastest, you know.' He hopped in the car and wound down the window. 'I'll see you later, Chloe.'

'Okay, Ryan.'

He drove down the dirt driveway, and in his rear-vision mirror he could see the little girl standing there watching him. She gave a sweet little wave, and only then did he realise how fast his heart was thumping in his chest.

Laura had the phone tucked beneath her ear as she whipped a bowl of egg whites and sugar. She watched as Ryan Gasper's dusty black sports car trawled down the bumpy front drive and turned right onto the main road away from town.

'You came visiting next door, Jill,' she accused down the phone, 'and you didn't even pop in here to say hello. Don't deny it. I saw your ute.'

'I had to get home to my cats,' Jill lied. 'So, have you spoken a reasonable word to him yet?'

'How can one be reasonable when one is caught singing to birds? Or when one is dressed in purple pants? Or when one is so outraged at being duped by some guy with more money than sense that one can barely speak English, much less reasonable English? Did you have any idea what he was cooking up with Cal?'

Jill's laughter echoed down the phoneline. 'Of course. I know everything. Now, don't tell me you are planning on hiding from him for the rest of your life.'

'Jill, he will not be here for the rest of anybody's life. Did you check out his clothes? All brand-new. All expensive. He doesn't belong out here.'

'I hardly noticed. Those bluer than blue eyes having

blinded me to much else,' Jill said. 'Except, of course, those glorious dark curls. My word!'

'Okay. I get where you're going with this. But, unlike you, I have no choice but to look past them. He's my Will's brother.'

Laura heard Jill's pause, and knew she wouldn't like what was coming next.

'Laura, I'm too old and cranky to let that slip through. I have *never* heard you call that young man *your* Will. Not when he was alive and traipsing after you like a lovesick puppy, and not since. What's up?'

Laura whisked all the harder, but said nothing.

'Don't look at this stranger and only imagine his back as he walks away, Laura. Not every man who comes into your life is going to leave you all alone.'

Laura stopped whisking and the mixing bowl sank to the bench. She put a hand to her temple to rub away the sudden spinning in her head. It seemed Jill was not going to be any use in relocating the man next door.

Laura peered out of the kitchen window but Chloe was out of her sight. Panic welled in her throat. How long had Chloe been gone? Her daughter knew better than not to check in every ten minutes or so. What if she fell ill? What if she got hurt? What if Ryan had found her scampering about outside, had seen his opportunity and taken her off in his dusty black car…?

The phone had begun to slip out of Laura's hand when suddenly Chloe came scurrying into the backyard with a tennis ball to throw for Chimp, who was busy sniffing a bunch of weeds in the corner of the yard.

She took a deep breath, swallowed down the huge lump of panic that had all but overwhelmed her, and rerouted the conversation before Jill took her to places she had no intention of going. 'Jill, this is one man I would be glad to see the back of. What if…what if he decides to contest for Chloe? What if his family decides they want to take her away from here? From me?'

'Then we will rain fire down upon him the likes of which he has never imagined. You are safe. Chloe is safe. Give yourself a break, and give the urban cowboy next door a break as well. The guy has no furniture, for goodness' sake. All he has is an old kettle, which one of your tradesmen must have left behind by mistake, and he's all alone out here—more alone than you have ever been. Face it, kiddo, he's a member of Chloe's family, a member of our little community, and neither I nor anyone else in Tandarah is going to disenfranchise him. We need men with brains and muscles to help in the fire season.'

Jill's words hit their mark. If she continued being so openly against Ryan it wouldn't do her any good. The people of Tandarah would take him under their wings, as they always did lost souls. And that was what he was. Laura had glimpsed hints of the hidden pain that he had not been able to cover up. Jill was on to something there.

This was a guy who was after more than a meet-and-greet with a new family member. But wondering how much more had Laura concerned to the point of sleepless nights. Until he had worked out his demons, in whatever way worked for him, it seemed she had no choice but to play happy neighbours and happy families with the slightly puzzled, entirely enigmatic *wunderkind* next door—or die trying.

Ryan took his time completing his pre-start, post-start, taxiing checks and run-ups. The local flight tower cleared his flight plan from the Mackay Airfield, east over Mount Bulla—which at this time of year would be dry and barren, without snow or the people snow brought to the region—then back around home again. A one-hour flight all up; it would be enough to get himself and Betsy used to the new run.

He took off, his back slamming into the seat with only a fraction of the power felt on a commercial flight, but the thrill was the same. The freedom. The comforting hum of the engine. The view of never-ending clear blue sky. There was nothing in the world like it.

He flew a large loop around the area, tilting his wing to check out the low lie of the local town, then crossed the hills and valleys of his new home. The house perched on top of the hill looked magnificent. Proud. The fact that it was to be his gave him an unexpected rush. The flush of ownership, of the challenge ahead. It had been so long since anything or anyone had challenged him the same way, and he found himself relishing it.

Maybe that was why he'd had such a love-hate relationship with his brother—his greatest challenger. The one person in his life who'd told him no on a regular basis. He missed that. He missed him. Perhaps even more so now. Will would have turned twenty-six this year, and Ryan wondered what sort of a man his brother would have become. Would fatherhood have changed him? Would it have forced him to take responsibility? If given the chance, would feisty Laura Somervale have made a man of him?

Ryan glanced down at the worker's cottage next door. From this height he only now realised how isolated Laura's place was. The next nearest house, bar his, was over the hill and far away—and she had lived out there for several years, raising a child on her own. Talk about a challenge.

Ryan circled the adjoining properties again, recognising the washing flapping on the cottage clothesline, and the spray of floral colour around the edge of the house. Her small fenced-in yard was neat and golden green, whereas the remainder of the surrounding landscape and the bulk of Kardinyarr looked barren and dry, as though her cottage was an oasis in the desert. After several minutes there was no sign of the lady of the house, and he was unexpectedly disappointed.

He tilted his wings back horizontal and headed back to the airstrip. He had plenty of work to do to get the staid old farm back into full working order. And spying on the nubile neighbour was not part of the plan. All he wanted from her was the chance to build a relationship with her daughter—and to wipe the smug smile from her face when his farm became a success.

That evening, as Laura pulled the washing off the line, she saw Ryan out on his back veranda, an old frayed workbook in one hand and a steaming mug in the other. Typical. All the men she had known would have lived on packet soup rather than learn to cook for themselves. Then she remembered Jill's comment that his furniture had not yet arrived, and that in fact he had no other choice.

She felt a tug of guilt as she remembered those first nights in the cottage on her own, after her father had passed away. Jill and other locals, people with families of their own to tend to, had run a constant line to her door with enough food to keep a cattle station full of people living for a month. Her whole life since then she had been passing on the favour, paying them back for their small kindnesses, and she planned to do so as long as she had strength in her cooking arm to do it.

That was what country people did, they looked out for

one another. Yet, knowing that, she had left Ryan rattling around in the big house with no word on when he would get to meet his niece. She was a horrible person, a horrible neighbour, and a horrible mother. Penance would be the only way through.

She remembered the cake she had baked earlier in the day for no reason in particular other than the need to cook. In a funny way the cake was Ryan's fault, and it was still sitting uneaten in her fridge.

Laura headed into the kitchen as Chloe came scampering into the room.

'What are you doing?'

'Making a peace-offering,' Laura said, tearing off a measure of cling-wrap and tucking it over the edge of a crockpot full of leftovers.

Chloe scrambled up onto the kitchen stool. Her nose crinkled. 'Is that Tuna Mornay? I *hate* Tuna Mornay.'

'Since when?' Laura asked.

'Since Tammy hates Tuna Mornay.'

Laura cracked a smile. 'Well, then, lucky for you, this Tuna Mornay is not for you.'

'Who's it for?'

'It's for Mr Gasper next door.'

'Oh, Uncle Ryan.'

Laura stopped her fussing and stared at her daughter. 'Excuse me?' she exclaimed, surprised any words had managed to slip through her suddenly rubbery lips. 'How did you come to call him by that name?'

Chloe's face dropped, as if she knew she had been caught out. 'He and I were talking this afternoon about Scotland, when I was, um, exorcising Chimp—'

'Exercising,' Laura corrected automatically. She clenched her hands to stop herself from throwing the

Tuna Mornay straight down the sink. 'What did he tell you, possum?'

'He said that he doesn't wear skirts.'

'Okay. But how do you come to call him Uncle Ryan?'

'Today at school Miss Tilda and some of the teachers were whispering about the fancy black car they had seen parked outside the Upper Gum Tree. I told Tammy I had seen that car next door, and Tammy said that her mum said that…'

Laura waved her hands in front of her face to stop the flourish of words. 'Okay, okay—I can see where this is going.'

So Ryan hadn't spilled the beans. The wonderful world of small-town gossip had got there first. *Stupid Laura!* She should have known. Though it had been so very long since she'd had to put up with any of that sort of guff, it simply had not occurred to her that Chloe might become a victim of the rumour mill. That had been a downright dangerous assumption—especially when concerning the emotional welfare of her child.

Laura ignored the food on the table, crouched down onto her haunches and looked her little girl in the eye, all the while laying a hand on her brow to check her temperature and watching the pace of her breathing with a practised eye. Everything seemed all right.

Now, how to explain all this to a six-year-old? *Here goes.* 'You know how you were asking me about cousins in Scotland yesterday, for your family-picture homework?'

Chloe nodded. 'I handed it in this morning.' Suddenly her bottom lip began to tremble.

'I know, possum. I know this is all very confusing.' The last thing she wanted was for her happy little girl to have undue stress brought upon her. She took Chloe's hand and led her to the couch.

'No, it's not. I get it. Ryan is my dad's brother. Come from a long way away because he wanted to meet me. Tammy explained all that. It's my picture.' She stopped for a little sniffle. 'I handed it in this morning. And when Tammy told me about Uncle Ryan I asked Miss Tilda for it back, so I could fix it. I told her it wasn't finished. But she said that I'd had time enough in the last week to get it done.'

Laura bit down on the run of nasty words that she wished to let forth. Miss Tilda was twenty years older than Laura, and twice her size, but she wouldn't know what hit her the next morning at school when the president of the PTA came to visit!

Laura ran a soothing palm over her daughter's golden curls. 'How about we have our own project instead? You can draw *me* a family picture, and you can put anyone in the picture you like. And, instead of this one being handed in to Miss Tilda, we can get it framed and we can hang it on the wall here.'

Chloe gulped down the last of her tears and her sniffles ceased. 'Framed?'

'You betcha! Now, let's back up a step. Mr Gasper says he doesn't wear a skirt? I don't know about that!'

Chloe's mouth twisted as she fought back a smile, and Laura's heart twisted right along with it. Laura had told Ryan that she and Chloe were perfectly happy on their own. Mostly that was true. But during those moments when her little girl was clever, or funny, or downright stupefying, Laura often found herself turning to share an adoring smile, a knowing wink, with someone who wasn't there.

'I'm heading over to Kardinyarr House now,' she said.

Chloe leapt down onto the floor and ran to the front door. 'Can I come with you?'

Laura smiled at her effervescent little girl, and said, 'Wherever you are is where I want to be.'

She followed Chloe outside to feed the guy-next-door, half hoping he would choke on her tuna and on her cake.

Ryan shifted his weight from one numb bottom cheek to the other. The hardwood stairs leading away from his back veranda weren't built for long sittings. He rubbed his eyes, encouraging them to refocus into the distance after a couple of hours of close reading.

The scuffle of boot on gravel caught his attention. He looked across the yard to find Laura coming towards him with Chloe tumbling and cartwheeling behind her. There was something slow and deliberate about her gait that had his wariness factor on full alert.

'Good evening, Mr Gasper,' she said, her voice low enough to set his nerves on edge.

'He likes to be called Ryan!' Chloe said.

'So I've heard,' his neighbour said, her eyes flaring. She then winked at her daughter, her face softening with affection, and Chloe grinned back. It was the first real smile he had seen Chloe give, and it was as though the sun had risen all over again.

'Ryan—or *Cowboy*. I'll answer to both,' Ryan interjected. Laura's eyes widened a fraction at his effrontery, but he just stared right back. She was simply going to have to get used to him. Especially since he had developed such an immediate fondness for her daughter, one he had every intention of cultivating. The food in Laura's arms suggested she was going to try to be civil. Unless, of course, it was laced with rat poison.

'Is that for me?' he asked.

'Jill told me you had nothing, and she would never forgive me if I let you starve to death. I've brought you a fork and a plate so you can eat now.'

'Why don't you come in and share it with me?' At her obvious reticence, the rat poison theory took hold. He stepped back against the doorway and waved an arm inside his home.

Chloe took a step forward, but Laura clicked her fingers and the little girl understood. With a world-class pout, she ran down the stairs and back to the cottage.

Laura's mouth tightened and her voice dropped to a whisper, even though her daughter was long since out of hearing range. 'I was going to invite you over for dinner tomorrow, to meet Chloe for real, but it seems the two of you have beaten me to the punch.'

Ha! Ryan didn't believe she had been planning to invite him anywhere—unless it was to take a long walk off a short plank. He reached down to take the plates from Laura's grip and laid them on the floor, out of reach. 'She found me. I was heading out, and suddenly she was just there, skipping. Apparently you had sent her outside so she couldn't listen in on your secret women's business with Jill.'

Her mouth dropped open, then snapped shut again. 'So it's my fault you met her without my permission, without my protection?'

The little kick in her voice ultimately sent him over the edge—the delicate, barely there, sizzling tone that made itself felt deep down inside of him. He hadn't done anything wrong through this whole process, but she made him feel as if he was treading on her toes at every step. All he'd asked was to meet Chloe—face to face, uncle to niece. The more she baulked, the more he would push his own case. 'Well, yes, Laura,' he said. 'It *was* entirely your fault.'

Her back stiffened, and her pouting lips thinned into a taut line. But the fire in her eyes could not be quenched. This woman was all heat, wavering from warmth and sunshine to spicy and ablaze. But there was no husband in the wings. Not even for the sake of her little girl. Surely there would be any number of strapping young farm boys willing to escort her to a country dance or two? Unless she still held a torch for a beau from long ago.

Ryan's stomach clenched painfully at the thought, and it blindsided him completely. Was that a pang of jealousy? Bad news. He had spent a lifetime dousing the envy he felt for the ease with which everything had come his brother's way—grades, offers, opportunities. He had no right to wonder if Laura had been as easy as everything else in Will's life. She was none of his business. Only Chloe was his business.

'I am not the enemy here,' he said, deciding it was in his best interests to be conciliatory. 'I know my presence is unexpected, but it was unexpected to me as well. In a parallel universe I would be on a plane right now, heading for Las Vegas, looking forward to a month's stay at a top hotel on the strip, all on the dollar of a major US bank. But instead I have made the choice to stay here.'

As he said it, he knew that it was true. He was going to make a go of Kardinyarr. For the sake of all the times he had told his brother no, this time he would stay for real. Better late than never? For the sake of the bruise obscuring his heart, he certainly hoped so.

'I'm staying, Laura. In order to get to know Chloe.

And to get to know you—the woman for whom my brother was willing to give up the world.'

Something shifted in Laura's uninterested and disbelieving countenance. A raw edge flashed across her expressive eyes. And there was his answer. Even the mention of Will's name gave her heartache. There was no danger in their continued acquaintance—not on her part, at least. So long as he could focus on Chloe alone, and disconnect himself from her mother's dominating energy, from the gentler pull of the passionate young girl in the fairy notepaper, he would be fine. They would all be fine.

He just had to be tough with himself. 'Come on in, Laura,' he said. 'I make a killer espresso.' So much for being tough with himself.

'Espresso?' she asked, one fine auburn eyebrow kicking into a point. It was sexy enough for him to need to draw new breath. Sexy? Where had *that* subversive little word come from? 'A regular cup of tea is more than enough to tempt this country soul.'

'Okay,' he said. 'So it's not really espresso. I plan to have a crack at plain old instant black coffee, made in an old kettle that has seen better days.'

She blinked. Once. Twice. And he thought perhaps she would acquiesce. He hoped she would. Maybe they could get to know each other a little better. Just two adults, sitting down and chatting…on the floor by his credenza…? But then she shook her head and took a step away.

'Another time, then?' Ryan offered. Laura sent him a tight smile but made no answer. Eventually, with a small wave, she left, following her daughter's path back to the cottage.

Ryan watched her the whole way—watched the sway

of her jeans-clad hips, the swing of her curled ponytail. He took in a deep breath and realised his heart-rate was flying. Every run-in with the woman had him feeling as if he had just drunk one of his favoured espressos.

The smell of the food got to him. He sat down on his back stairs and ate the delicious tuna concoction straight from the bowl as the sun set over his property—while trying to convince himself he was not acting like some teenager with an inappropriate crush.

CHAPTER FIVE

THE next day at school Laura worked up a perfectly good head of steam, tracked down Miss Tilda, explained a thing or two about Chloe's family situation, then accepted a job catering for Miss Tilda's upcoming birthday celebrations, quoting a price that would barely make her a profit. She was a sucker, no doubt about it.

'Laura Somervale! Just the woman I was looking for.' Jesse Bunton—Cal's wife and Tammy's mother—popped her head through the car window just as Laura was about to pull away.

'Morning, Jesse,' Laura said through a stiff smile. 'My daughter has been telling stories about you.'

'Oh,' Jesse said, bringing a hand to her innocent heart. 'I hope they're all good.'

'Not really. I realise the whole town knows about my new neighbour. But can I trust you to pass on the word to be careful about what Chloe and her friends overhear? I don't need her to be upset by anything, or anyone.'

'Oh, of course,' Jesse blustered. 'If I ever inadvertently said anything to make our little Chloe anxious I would never forgive myself.'

Laura nodded her thanks, knowing the word would be all over town, quick-smart, that she was on the warpath against any sort of gossip that made its way to the classroom. But she also knew by the twinkle in the school mum's eye that she wasn't off the hook. 'Was there something else, Jesse?'

'Well, since you brought him up, we were hoping to find out a little more about that new neighbour of yours.'

'Who's we?' Laura asked, peering past Jesse to find half a dozen other local school mums inching into a circle around her.

'Spill, Laura!' one called out, gaining confidence. 'What's he like?'

'Is he straight?' Jesse asked. 'Is he single? Is he staying?'

Considering they were all married, she didn't know what the big deal was. Well, okay. She knew. Ryan Gasper was gorgeous. He was empirically, undeniably gorgeous. Compared with the usual assortment of tubby, balding, old-before-their-time lot who lived within a twenty-kilometre radius, Ryan Gasper was a rare dreamboat. A rare dreamboat who had invited her in for coffee the evening before, and for a brief moment there had been something in his eyes that had made her think he was after more than a companion for hot beverages. But for her to be even thinking that he might see her that way was ridiculous. Dangerous, detrimental to achieving the 'happy neighbour' relationship she had decided she would need to foster, and ridiculous.

'Apart from the fact that he is Chloe's uncle, and that he has bought Kardinyarr,' she said, keeping her voice even, 'all I know is that he won't say no to free food.'

Perhaps that was playing a tad unfair. Once that snippet of news got around he would have more visitors than he would know what to do with. He would barely have time to leave the kitchen, much less come a-visiting the house across the way. Laura bit back a wicked smile.

'So you've had dinner with him already?' Jesse said, sending a meaningful grin to the others. 'Good for you!'

'Well, no,' Laura backtracked. 'I've baked him Tuna Mornay and a chocolate cake, but that's all.'

'So he's tried one of your cakes? The guy has no chance!' The ladies all laughed along with Jesse.

'No. Uh-uh. You've got the wrong idea…' But with every sentence she was digging a deeper hole for herself. They were as bad as Jill, matchmaking in their spare time. And if this lot were happy to say it to her face, she wondered what the rest of the town were saying behind her back. All she could do was continue supplying no ammunition for their ideas; they would realise her life was as conventional as theirs, and talk would fizzle. She had discovered that, in time, it always did.

'Do stop by at my place when you visit Kardinyarr,' she said, before gunning the engine and heading off.

Ryan spent the morning getting dirty at the Minbah livestock markets. He trawled the unique bazaar from one end of the car park to the other. Families sold every mower part one could ever need out of the back of Kombi vans. Local kids manned tables full of their old toys, selling them off without remorse or entanglement at a dollar a piece. The cocktail scent of human sweat and animal waste was indiscriminate, but the energy of the place more than made up for it.

The livestock auction was held in a square wooden barn, taller than it was wide, with a dressage ring in the centre, surrounded on three sides by slap-hazard rows of wooden seats rising to a man's height from the roof. Ryan spent some time talking to a couple of vendors, and made himself known to Doc Larson, the local veterinarian, before deciding on the mix of beasts he wanted, and by the time their place in the queue was reached his palms were damp with nerves.

The room was stifling, the crowd noisy, but the auction process was meticulous.

This is what it's all about, Ryan thought. Buying and selling. Market forces. Capitalist economics. This was exactly what he had been talking about for the last twenty years without ever having lived it at the most elementary level.

Arriving back at Kardinyarr, he was eager to harness his enthusiasm—and the surplus of ideas regarding international trade and primary industry rocketing through his mind. He grabbed his laptop and went to make himself a cup of coffee, then realised that, though he had enough powdered milk to last him three months without a fridge, he hadn't bought any coffee or any sugar. So, with a mug filled with crisp, tinny tank water, he sat on the back steps, his laptop resting on the step above, and set to getting his thoughts down.

The next two hours flew. His fingers were cramped from pounding the keyboard with more vigour than he ever had before. *And* he was starving.

Before he had the chance to change his mind, he grabbed the empty Tuna Mornay tray—the cake tin still held enough of the heavenly cake for him to keep hold of it a little longer—then he jogged out through the back door and across the patch of grass that led him to the cottage next door.

He passed by an overturned bicycle, Chloe's discarded skipping-rope, and the washing line with newly washed clothes hanging damp and long in the hot, heavy, windless air. He cleared his throat and knocked on the open back door. 'Anyone home?'

He could hear noises from inside the house, music playing quietly on a stereo—he recognised it as 'In the Hall of the Mountain King', from *Peer Gynt*—and kitchen noises, cooking noises. And then the smell hit him. Sugar. Fruit. Pastry. He drank deeply of the most delicious mix of smells he had ever known.

Intrigued, he opened the unlocked fly-screen door and entered. The small entrance was cluttered. Several pairs of Chloe's shoes were piled up in the corner, and a square of mud-splattered welcome rug encouraged him to wipe his feet. A hall table littered with mail—some opened, some not—held a huge vase of dried wild flowers in the centre, all but hiding an antique mirror residing behind it. Several mismatched photo frames littered what was left of the table space. He'd leaned in to have a closer look when the lady of the house popped her head around the doorway.

'Ryan!' she called. 'I thought I heard somebody.'

He snapped up straight, sprung snooping, his feet scuffling on the floor like a naughty schoolboy. 'I hope you don't mind. I let myself in.'

He held out the casserole dish and she took it.

'You may as well have the grand tour now that you've made it past the guard dog,' she said.

Ryan followed Laura's line of sight to find a miniature fox terrier snuffling at the toecaps of his boots. He squatted down and offered his hand to the creature for a smell. After a few tentative sniffs the dog's body began to wriggle, and he earned himself a happy yap. 'Who's this?' Ryan called out.

'Chimp,' Laura said from further away. 'We should be a registered zoo, with the odd assortment of animals we've adopted over the years. It's one of the many nice things about living on so much land.'

Ryan followed her voice. Rounding the small entranceway, he found himself in the body of the house. An overstuffed floral lounge suite filled the living space.

A dining-room table was littered with trays, muffin cups, and sheets of aluminium foil. A record player—an actual old-style record player—rocked gently in one corner, spilling Grieg through a pair of ancient mission-brown speakers. An open-plan kitchen with a window overlooked Laura's undulating land and their shared front driveway. A doorway led to what must have been the bedrooms and bathroom.

It was…cosy. Warm. Snug. But it was about a quarter of the size of his new home, and smaller even than some of the serviced apartments he had been put up in when in some of the larger cities. The Vegas hotel room he had given up would have fitted her house twice, and he would have been staying there alone.

'Why Chimp?' he asked, skirting around a rug with a rocking-chair in the corner until he came up against the kitchen bench.

Laura switched off the tap and dried her hands on her apron. 'Chloe's wanted a chimpanzee since the day she first saw one on television.'

Ryan followed the wave of her hand to find what must have been a twenty-year-old black and white box on top of a lamp-table against the wall. The thing was so old it was probably worth more now to a collector than it would have been when first bought.

'After some negotiating a couple of Christmases ago,' Laura continued, 'we settled on a pup named Chimp.' She shot him a glance warmed by memories of her daughter. 'Now, come to think of it, I would put money on the fact that Chloe always wanted a dog and used all the leverage she could muster.'

'Clever girl, eh?'

'You have no idea.'

A familiar click and whir filled the silence as the needle went back to the beginning of the record. Ryan simply waited, looking over the woman before him as though time stood still between songs.

Silhouetted by the sunlight spilling through the wide kitchen window, Laura looked as alluring as all-get-out. Again, she wore a dress, pale blue this time, with a floaty skirt, tight middle, and thin shoulder straps. A plain white apron was pulled tight around her waist, cinched at the back in a large bow. Her clear brown eyes, the colour of bushland grass after a long drought, looked back at him—steady, strong, unwavering.

No wonder Will had been smitten. Even at eighteen she would have been something else to behold. She was undeniably the most unashamedly feminine woman Ryan had ever met—all soft curves and curling hair, with long limbs and a pretty face, smooth lips, skin quick to blush. Yet she had a complicated mind and a smart mouth that grabbed him deeper than her merely aesthetic delights ever could.

A faint crackle heralded the beginning of the record and the fine strains of Grieg released Ryan from his consideration of Laura's entirely natural loveliness.

'Chloe's at school still,' she told him, her voice slightly wavering.

Was she nervous, having him alone in her house? Rather than sending him running it made him all the more determined to stay. 'I knew that.'

'So why did you come over?' she asked more slowly. 'Just to bring back the Tuna Mornay dish?'

You wish. He bit back his response and searched for a reason that would make her relax. He retraced his steps. Out of her warm kitchen. Away from her cluttered entrance. Outside of her inviting doorway. Back to his empty house with his half-empty pantry. 'I was hoping to borrow some sugar.'

He expected to be shot down in flames by some entirely deserved barb from a woman who knew how to deliver them. But instead she laughed. Her slender throat worked as the delightful tinkle of laughter escaped her throat. 'You're kidding me.'

'I'm not,' he continued with a shrug. 'I don't know that I have ever shopped before for groceries enough to fill a pantry, and I overcompensated on odd things, like flour, and forgot basic things like coffee and eggs.'

'That's priceless,' she said, her laughter gone, but her face still creased by a smile. 'Now, go on and sit.'

After the moments it took for him to disengage himself from her unexpected warmth, he looked around for the dog.

'Chimp is outside, chasing the magpies,' she said. 'I was talking to you, Ryan. Sit. Stay. I'll make you a proper coffee.'

Not daring to push his luck, he pulled up a kitchen stool and sat, leaning his elbows against the bench and trying to quell his suddenly growling stomach. 'So, what's with all the aluminium foil?' he asked, motioning to her flour-covered apron and the two dozen trays littering her workspace.

'Tonight is a get-together of the local chapter of the Country Fire Association.'

'Is there any local group for which you are not a volunteer?'

She shrugged. 'I do what I can. I am not entirely philanthropic; I've been hired to cook for this event as well.'

'Is catering really that lucrative?'

At that statement she stared him down. 'I more than *cater*, Mr Gasper,' she said, her voice overbrimming with confidence. 'I can do things with sugar and flour that you have never experienced. Even in your big-city cafés.'

'Maybe you've been into the wrong cafés. I'm sure I could show you a couple that would blow your mind.'

'Could you, now?'

'Why not?' he said, feeling as if he was pushing against some sort of diminishing boundary. 'Maybe one day I'll take Chloe into town for a play date, and maybe we'll invite you along.'

She watched him from behind her long lashes. 'Well, maybe I'll accept your invitation,' she said. She turned back to the sink and began washing out a bowl full of strawberries, and he decided then and there that he liked it much better when they were moving towards each other than when she was pulling away. 'So, when were you last in a big-city café?'

After a brief pause she turned back to face him, wiped her wet hands on her apron, cocked a hip against the bench and looked him straight in the eye. 'It was the day of your brother's funeral. I had some time before my train was due to take me home and I had a sudden need for piles of chocolate. The just as strong need to be out of the rain meant that I stumbled into the first open café I found. The pastries were fair, but I knew I could do better.'

Listening to her talk about that day, Ryan felt a deep hard pressure against his lungs, festering, compounding, until he could think of nothing else. She was so cool and tough, but Ryan had to fight the desperate need to clear his throat and look away.

'So why weren't you there?' she asked.

'Where?' he asked, his voice regrettably ragged, but he knew what she meant.

'At Will's funeral.'

Ryan searched through the array of possible answers. He'd been busy. He hadn't been able to get a flight in time. It had been too late to pull out of his commitments in Paris.

'I was angry with him,' he said, surprised at the words spilling from his own mouth.

He ran fingers over the pale scars on his knuckles, formed when he had smashed the window in his hotel room. His chest again grew tight with memories, and tighter still as he awaited her response. Would that be the end of it? Would she never more look at him with those brief flashes of inescapable curiosity, as if she wanted to know more, to know him deeper, as he wanted to know her? Would she write him off completely for being so callous?

But, instead, she gave him an accepting smile and said, 'I know *exactly* what you mean.' Jill was right; Laura was far too kind for the likes of him.

'When my dad died suddenly, a few years ago, I was furious,' she explained. 'I was so angry with him for leaving me alone, for not giving me the chance to let him know how much I was going to miss him. And I was angry with all the good people of Tandarah because, in my blinkered grief, I knew they couldn't possibly know how I felt. Most of all, I was angry with myself for being so angry. I am a pretty happy-go-lucky person, but during those first weeks I thought I would never remember how to be happy again.'

An easy smile slid across her face, and he knew that those feelings had long since been reconciled. Despite being a single mother, living from hand to mouth, she was in a much better place than he was.

'Tell me a nice memory you have of Will,' she said, as though sensing his melancholy.

A nice memory, eh? They'd clashed so often, he wondered if he could. He shuffled through his memories for something he thought Laura would appreciate.

'When he was a kid,' he said at length, 'he would lie out on the trampoline, staring at the stars, until somebody remembered he was out there and dragged him back inside.' He shook his head, diffusing the memory. 'I always wanted to light a fire under him, to get him animated, but at the same time I envied him that level of serenity.'

'Chloe can look through picture books for hours on end,' Laura interjected. 'I *never* had that sort of patience at her age. I still don't. I constantly have to be moving, doing something, talking, walking, cooking or singing, for fear if I stop I might never want to get started again.'

'Yep. I've been there.'

'But Chloe has the ability to simply *be*. As did Will.' She shrugged. 'It's a gift.'

The more he knew about her, the more Ryan believed Laura was the one with the gift. She had an amazing resilience, and an ability to smile through anything. 'How did you get past the anger?' he asked.

'Too hot bubble bath therapy went a long way,' she said, with a cheeky twinkle in her eye, before turning back to her strawberries.

The sudden image of Laura in a deep spa bath, her hair pinned high on her head, damp curls stuck to her neck as she lay up to her chest in bubbles, was enough to have Ryan shift himself on the seat. 'Enlighten me.'

'Happy to. The first thing you should know is that the joys of the too hot bubble bath are all in the timing.'

'All in the timing,' Ryan repeated, committing the information and the accompanying image to memory.

'For example, a couple of months ago I was down by the dam, reeling in the hose after watering my plum trees, when I was caught in a sudden sun shower. By the time I made it back up to the house I was soaked through. What better way to warm up than with a too hot bubble bath?'

Now Ryan had to fight off the image of Laura running through the rain, her clothes soaked to her skin, sun glinting off her hair. 'Tell me more.'

Laura glanced over her shoulder at the sound of his suddenly uneven voice, but when he merely smiled politely back, she continued.

'Okay... Ummm... When I dropped Chloe off at her first ever day at school, I came home to find I had nothing to do. No dinners to cater, no phone calls to make, no clothes to wash. Nothing. After a too hot bubble bath, I got back into my pyjamas and ate nothing all day but half a round of brie, an entire block of chocolate and left over, two-day-old, reheated fried rice. That was perfect timing.'

She spun to face him, her skirt twirling before settling in soft folds about her legs. She took a bite of a strawberry, her teeth biting down and her lips drawing the succulent flesh into her mouth. She threw the stem into the sink, licked her fingers, then continued, wholly unaware of Ryan's escalating enchantment.

'Oh, and then there was one beautiful afternoon I discovered the consummate hanging-washing-on-the-line soundtrack. I sang along with every song; the magpies weren't so impressed, but I had a ball. Suddenly through the damp white sheets I caught sight of a perfect cerulean blue sky and thought, Why have I been looking down all day? *Voila!* Perfect timing.'

Ryan laughed aloud as he realised how the conversation had turned. 'But, from what I remember, on that day some stranger bundled up in shiny boots and a not-so-shiny car and threw a spanner in the works.'

'That he did.' She nodded, her eyes sparkling. 'And, alas, that perfect time was lost for ever.' She smiled, creating an adorable dimple in her right cheek, and suddenly Ryan thought of Chloe. The little girl who had the same dimple. His brother's child.

He sucked in a cooling breath. What was he doing, allowing himself to become so captivated by a woman who had shared his brother's bed? The problem was, he couldn't help himself. There was something about her that had him entranced, intrigued, covetous of any feelings she had ever had for any other man.

'Sincerest apologies,' he said, meaning it. He wished he had never denied this dazzling woman a moment's pleasure.

'Apology accepted,' she said, something in the timbre of her voice making him think she wasn't wholly unaware of his train of thought. 'But only because that is the beauty and the bane of the too hot bubble bath. I revere it all the more for its rarity.'

'Thank you for sharing that with me.'

'No biggie.' She lifted a shoulder, then her gaze sharpened as she pointed a finger at him. 'But it wasn't only too hot bubble baths that helped me cope. If your bother had not turned up when he did, if he had not been willing to listen to my blathering with an outsider's kind ear, it might have been a very different story.'

Again, Ryan's gut kicked with a horrible stab of foolish envy. *Next subject.* 'So, how are you going to prove to this city boy that you are such a cook?' he asked.

'The chocolate cake and Tuna Mornay weren't enough?'

'Not even close,' he lied. The memory of the flavours and textures had his tastebuds watering in response.

She smiled again, drawn in by his challenge. 'How do mini-mincepies and chocolate-covered strawberries sound?'

'It sounds like a goal well worth shooting for.'

She reached over and grabbed the percolator from inside a cupboard. 'And coffee, right? Black with sugar?'

Seeing that she had no bench space left on which to put the coffeepot, Ryan snapped to attention. He leapt off the stool and was by her side in a flash. 'The one thing I can make is a cup of coffee. So, you do your magic over there, and I will make a brew. Deal?'

Big amber eyes blinked up at him, and Ryan had a funny feeling that nobody had ever offered to make her coffee in her own home before. Any man would be lucky to have this creature waiting for him at home, all wrapped up so sweet in one of her cotton dresses, but he had the growing feeling she had never been spoilt as she deserved to be.

But what if he had known Laura back then? If he had done as Will had asked and come to Kardinyarr and seen the reason why Will had been willing to give up Oxford, to reject Paris, would he have understood? Would he have left Will to his own devices and stopped pushing? Or would he have taken one look at young Laura Somervale and flipped over her himself? He kicked himself for never making room for the possibility that his brother might be onto something good for himself until it was too late.

Damn Will for dying! Ryan thought. *Damn him for leaving this woman all alone. And damn him for creating such a captivating picture of this woman, and this place, in his e-mails that the minute Sam showed them to me I had had no choice but to come all the way out to the middle of nowhere to see what the fuss was all about.*

He reached out and took a hold of the percolator and coffee bag. His fingers brushed against hers for a fraction of a second and she jerked away as though burnt. Desperate to find somewhere to put her hands, she bunched her fingers into fists at her sides then flattened them against her skirt. It was enough to make him long to touch her again. How would she react if he brushed his knuckles along the smooth curve of her cheekbone…?

'Coffee would be…helpful,' she said, taking a step back towards the sink, her voice unbelievably husky as she looked into his eyes. 'Thank you.'

Ryan nodded and did as he was asked. But as soon as the hot water and coffee were happily becoming acquainted, he turned and leant his back against her bench, watching her knead out a slab of freshly mixed pastry. Her back was to him as she finished off the food portion of their meal, and he soon became entranced by the big white bow of her apron. All he had to do was reach out and grab one end, and the whole thing would slip undone…

She glanced over her shoulder and caught him staring. Her wheat-gold eyes flashed, her soft cheeks warmed, and it was all he could do to stop himself from dragging her into his arms and kissing her until her pupils became dark and heavy and her limbs grew languid. He watched, fascinated, as she swallowed down a great lump in her throat, and her eyelashes battered against her cheeks. At length, her gaze tore from his and landed upon the bubbling percolator. She reached out for it as though it was a lifeline.

'Uh-uh,' he chastised. 'That's my job.' When she didn't move, he gave her a little bump with his hip and she skittered back to the safety of the sink. 'So, my part of the cooking deal is almost done, how about you?'

He risked a glance and found her watching him, her gaze hooded, her thoughts far away. But she blinked and was back with him before he knew it.

She tried a smile, but it went no further than her pale pink lips. 'Sure. Of course.' Wiping her hands on her apron again, she then slipped on a pair of oven mitts and opened up the top oven.

The mix of aromas that hit Ryan knocked him for six. 'That smells incredible.'

The smile lighting her profile this time was real. 'My own mince pie recipe. The secret ingredient is the plums.'

'Well, it's not a secret any more.'

'Are you going to be making them any time soon?'

'Ah, no. Even if I did have the utensils, I wouldn't have a clue what else to put in, bar the plums, so your secret is safe with me.'

'That's what I figured.'

'Hey,' he said rounding on her with arms crossed across his chest. 'I'll have you know that I can cook a very little.'

'What's your speciality? Three-minute noodles? Egg on toast? Frozen pizza?'

'Actually, all of the above. Plus a couple that you will never know about.'

'Oh, and why's that?' Her smile now reached her eyes, and he swore there was now an almost flirtatious swing in her hips as she carried the pies past his straining nose and over to the edge of the sink.

'Because you are laughing at me,' he said, watching her every move with extra attention. 'So now you will just have to lie awake at night trying to guess.'

'Ryan, I can assure you the minute my head hits the pillow I will be fast asleep. You moving in next door will do nothing to change that. Shall we eat outside?' she asked, loading another tray of pies into the oven before placing a few on a white dish for them to enjoy.

Ryan glanced around the busy room. 'Either there or on the floor.'

'If you insist on being churlish you'll get nothing.'

This time Ryan had to lick his lips they were so suddenly dry. 'Off to bed without supper?' he asked.

Her face dropped, as though she'd only just realised that they had in fact been flirting outrageously for some time. But he wasn't going to let her off the hook again. It was her turn.

'I am a mother,' she said by way of apology. 'Sorry. I find myself telling off the local vet if he doesn't wipe his feet at the front door. It's pathological.'

It's adorable, Ryan thought, but he knew that saying it aloud would only strain the capricious confidence that had begun to blossom between them.

'Bring the coffee?' she requested over her shoulder.

Ryan did as he was told, and followed her through the front door and out to the portico where a wrought-iron table and chairs sat in one corner by a pretty garden sprouting with new flowers.

'Yoo-hoo!'

Their two heads snapped in the direction of Ryan's front door. It seemed he had a visitor.

'Oh. That's Jesse. Cal Bunton's wife,' Laura said, her

voice and her eyes so filled with regret Ryan bit back a curse. 'I kind of told her that you were in need of feeding.'

'Mr Gasper!' Jesse called out, her voice coming louder and closer. 'Don't be shy. I know you're here. I can see your divine car!'

'You should go,' Laura said, her arms still filled with the tray of delicious pies. 'We can do this another time.'

His mouth twitched. He knew exactly why she had told Jesse Bunton he needed feeding. To keep him busy so she wouldn't have to. He had stupidly been thinking she was flirting, when the whole time she had been politely marking time until somebody else took him off her hands.

He pulled away to stand in the bright sunshine of her front yard, leaving her shaded in the doorway. He imagined she looked sad, disappointed to be sending him away. But he was a wilful man, and in his life he had imagined many things that simply weren't there.

'Thanks for the almost-lunch, Laura. It was enlightening,' he said, before turning and jogging away.

Over the next couple of hours the line of cars, utes and four-wheel drives kicking up dust on their communal driveway was out of control. Laura didn't know whether to be thankful that she had brought the town's women to Ryan's rescue, or if she wanted to wind back the clock and see what might have happened if Jesse hadn't blundered along.

That night the Country Fire Association was going to have a feast the likes of which they had never seen: glazed tartlets, homemade jam doughnuts, Pavlova piled high with fresh fruit and whipped cream, all things sweet and succulent. Anything that might help whisk away the disturbing tension coursing through her overripe body.

Something had been cooking between Ryan and her. Something friendly—and more than neighbour-friendly. But, alas, her own hubris in daring the local women to come out to Kardinyarr and see that nothing was happening between them had ended up preventing something happening between them.

Of course that was for the best. Being hospitable towards Chloe's uncle was one thing, but being *friendly* was another. It didn't matter that she was undeniably drawn to his easy confidence. It didn't matter that every time she felt his eyes upon her she warmed from the inside out. It didn't matter because she knew Ryan had come to Kardinyarr in search of family, not in search of a complicated connection with the mother of his newfound niece.

Laura thought back to the last time she had spent concentrated time in a man's company. She had cherished Will for the comfort he had given her when she'd needed it most, but she had never felt as if she was walking on hot coals whenever he came within five feet of her.

Will's shrewd big brother was in a whole other league. Where Will had been a young man, all at sea, Ryan was a man of action who knew exactly what he wanted and made no bones about going after it. But what had that afternoon been all about if it hadn't been about him letting her know in a million subtle ways that he wanted her? A touch here. A look there. A delicious shiver ran down Laura's spine until she scrunched her toes into the floor mat below her bare feet. There was something about him that meant so long as he was sleeping in the house next door she would never again fall asleep the minute her head hit the pillow.

By the time she had taken up every spare surface in her lounge room, with twice as much food as the CFA could possibly eat, a pair of moving trucks had trundled up the dirt drive. Through the window, she watched Ryan jog over to meet the trucks. There was much back-slapping and laughter as he set to, helping the men carry piles of furniture into Kardinyarr House. Laura saw a bed for each room, at least a dozen dining chairs, lounge suites for both the formal lounge and the sitting room…

Did that really mean he was thinking of staying? Her heart leapt. She slapped it down. But it was too late. Dangerous feelings had crept up on her when she was determinedly looking the other way. She wanted him to stay, for if he left now she would miss him. She would miss the look in his eye when he spoke of his brother, the way he listened when she prattled, the way he watched her when he thought she wasn't paying attention.

Damn Jill and her meddling, Laura thought. *Damn Will for building Ryan up so brilliantly in my imagination. And damn Ryan himself for the little-boy-lost look in his eyes, and for making me believe that somehow I am the only one who can help him find whatever it is he is looking for…*

CHAPTER SIX

'CHLOE!' Laura called out later that night, when dinner was almost on the table. Her ears pricked for a loud, frustrated *Wha-a-at?* But the response did not come.

'Chloe!' she called again, louder this time. Still nothing. Her chest constricted. Chloe knew not to go further than calling distance, and she knew why—especially when the flowers were in bloom, the ground was more dust than soil, and when the wind had picked up more than a whisper.

Laura jogged through the house, checking each room as she went, but Chloe was nowhere to be seen. She ran out of the house and called across the gully. She strained her ears to hear her daughter's voice, to pick up a noise, a scent, anything, her instincts stretched to their limits. And then she heard it. Laughter. Coming from the direction of Kardinyarr.

Her heart thudding against her ribs, Laura found Ryan crouched by a fence halfway down the hill, hammer in hand, fixing a broken paling. Chloe stood by him, holding onto a tin of nails, chattering away blithely about her day at school. Chimp lay next to a new red toolbox, munching on an old bone. While Ryan concentrated on not putting a nail through his thumb he listened, looking Chloe's way every few moments, and asking questions every time her speech came to a halt.

Laura watched as Ryan held out a hand for a nail, holding up his thumb and forefinger to show Chloe the size he was after. With her tongue half hanging out of her mouth, Chloe scoured the tray until she found the right one, and when Ryan grinned his thanks she just glowed.

Laura's heart lurched. Troubled as she was by her own mixed-up feelings towards Ryan Gasper, she hadn't thought this whole thing through to its logical conclusion. Of course Chloe would fall for the guy. She'd never had a solid male influence in her life, and then one day this prime specimen fell from the sky into her lap. Laura sensed a whole heap of trouble brewing. If—no, *when*, Ryan headed back to his real life, Chloe would be too young to understand why she had been left behind.

'Chloe,' Laura called out, her voice gruff. Her daughter jumped out of her skin. 'Didn't you hear me calling you?'

Ryan stood and turned from his work to face her. Her blood warmed instantly at the sight of him, dressed down in an unfamiliar chocolate-coloured T-shirt, snug, shabby button-fly jeans, aged sneakers, and a red baseball cap worn backwards the better to see his work at hand. Beads of sweat lay across his brow, between clumping, damp dark curls, and his skin already looked a shade more tanned from the kiss of a couple of days of sun.

Laura growled at herself and tore her disobedient gaze away from the man to the imperilled little girl at his side. She put her hands on her hips, raised an eyebrow, and waited for Chloe to explain herself.

'I was outside the back door playing when I heard Ryan's hammer. I asked if I could help and he said that was fine.' Chloe looked to her partner in crime for reassurance, and he came to the rescue.

'Without my little helper here I'm sure this job would

have taken me twice as long.' He ruffled Chloe's curls and she beamed up at him.

Laura turned on him. 'That's all well and good. But your little *helper* here has a deal with her *mother*. Don't you, Miss Chloe?'

Chloe bowed her head, her tiny shoulders slumping. 'When at home I am not to go any further than shouting distance, or I have to check in every ten minutes.' Then her head sprang up. 'But I was with Uncle Ryan! So if my breathing became bad he would have helped me.'

Ryan's gaze flicked from mother to daughter. 'Your breathing?' he repeated.

'Chronic asthma,' Chloe explained, mimicking the words of her many doctors. 'If I have an attack, I could die. My asthma is so bad even with regular use of my reliever and preventer puffers nothing is certain.'

Ryan pushed away from the fence, as though distancing himself from Chloe's dire words. 'I… Really? She did mention asthma the other day, but I had no idea it was that serious.'

'I just need her to be nearby. To know she is safe,' Laura snapped. 'You understand now why I have tried to take my time with all of *this*?' She waved her hand about, taking in him, her, and the house behind them. *Don't mess about playing happy families with my little girl unless you mean it.*

Ryan's sneaker-clad foot kicked at a lonely tuft of grass. 'Yeah,' he said, the word emerging slowly from his mouth. 'Yeah.'

He looked so appalled, and Laura felt instantly guilty for being so abrupt. It wasn't his fault that Chloe hadn't followed the rules. It wasn't his fault that Chloe had flitted to him like a moth to a flame. It wasn't his fault that both Somervale women were becoming dangerously used to the fact of him being there.

'She hasn't had a full-blown attack in months,' Laura said, softening her temper. 'So long as we take care she might never again.'

He reached out and laid a gentle protective hand across Chloe's shoulders. 'Just don't go so far again without letting your mum know, okay?' he said.

Chloe leant into his embrace and Laura fought the cry of anguish that rose in her throat. Instead, she held out her hand and Chloe tumbled over into her arms for a forgiving hug.

I am sorry, Ryan mouthed over Chloe's head.

It's not your fault, Laura mouthed back.

Ryan tore the cap from his head, wiped at the sweat on his forehead with the back of his gloves, then tugged the cap back on the right way around. Gloves.

'Where on earth did you find those?' she asked, her sudden outburst drawing all eyes to Ryan's gloved hands.

He held out his hands palm-up. 'I found them in the front shed. Are they yours?'

'No. They were my father's,' Laura said, her voice sounding as though it was coming from far away. She reached out and ran a finger along Ryan's open palm, the sensation of worn old suede so familiar. 'Funny, I looked for them everywhere after he died.'

'Would you like them back?'

Laura shook her head. 'No. I'm just happy to know that they're still about, still working on Kardinyarr's fences. He ran cattle on Kardinyarr land right up until the heart attack took him.'

'Then I guess there is symmetry in the fact that these

old gloves are still achieving the same ends today,' he offered, his voice soft and kind.

'Mmm, and a day of working those fences without gloves and your girly-soft city-boy hands would never be the same again.'

Ryan's strong gloved fingers suddenly closed over her own soft hand. 'You do enjoy taunting me, don't you, Ms Somervale? I think it comes as naturally to you as breathing.'

Laura's cheek twitched. 'I'm afraid it does.' Taunting him felt darned good. Fighting with him gave her more of an endorphin rush than laughing with almost anybody else. Sparring with him made her feel wilful, resilient, fascinating. It had been a long time since she had felt that way about herself.

Chloe clearing her throat broke the exquisite mood that had settled over the two of them. 'Can we finish the fence now you're here?' Chloe asked. 'I do have other things to do, you know!'

Laura coughed back a laugh. The girl was barely six, yet she was already showing signs of becoming a right little teenager. Laura was not looking forward to the day Chloe discovered boys were for kissing rather than for swapping footy cards and collecting tadpoles. As such, she slid her hand from Ryan's rough grasp.

'What do you have to do tonight?' Laura asked, and Chloe backed down enough to look sheepish.

'Miss Tilda said that my letter As need work. I didn't like her saying that in front of all the other kids. So by the end of term I plan to have the best letter As in the whole class.'

Ryan and Laura shared a smile, and again it hit her exactly how much she missed not having someone in her life to share moments like these. Special, unique

Chloe moments. Chloe's first word. Chloe's first step. The first terrifying midnight rush to the doctor when she'd thought Chloe would never take breath again. These were moments she had lived through alone. Jill had heard everything after the fact, in their daily phone chats, but it wasn't the same. Having someone else to bear witness felt terribly precious.

Dangerous, she corrected. Because though this man was invested, though it was likely he would be in their lives from this day on, it would be on the periphery. Somehow, she was no longer afraid that Ryan would try to take Chloe from her. Despite her warnings to herself she totally trusted him. But now she felt the cold curl of dread for the day he *would* leave them both.

'Chloe, how about you head in now and practise your As. I'm sure Ryan won't mind.'

'But who will get the nails for him?' Chloe asked.

'Your mum can do that,' Ryan offered promptly.

Laura had been about to say he was a big boy and could handle himself, but now she was caught. 'Of course I will, possum,' she said. 'Now, off you go. We'll be done here in a minute.'

'Okay!' Chloe cried out, before skipping happily back to the house, with a less energetic Chimp sniffling along in her wake.

Laura spun to lean on the fence a good arm's distance from Ryan. The sounds of evening whispered in her ear. This was her favourite time of day. Right when the sun had disappeared beneath the hill, the brilliant orb having reached out its last gasp of too bright light, casting a kaleidoscope of colour across the undulating horizon. The tall, fine eucalypts on the next hill cast disproportional shadows into the gully below. The temperature dropped five degrees in as many minutes. Night was close on sunset's heels.

She glanced sideways to find Ryan looking out over the land with the same wistful expression.

'Nice outfit,' she said, having to break the loaded silence.

Ryan looked down to his scuffed shoes, then back up at her with a crooked grin. 'What? These old things?'

He looked so darned good in those old things her breath hitched and she had to look away. 'Did you raid the second-hand store in town?' she asked.

'Nah. Along with furniture and appliances, my sister Sam packed up some old clothes stored in my apartment in Melbourne. You like?'

She shrugged. There was certainly no need for him to know quite how much she liked. 'In that get-up you could almost pass for a local.'

'I'll take that as a compliment.' He grinned and held out two fingers about an inch apart. 'I would like a nail this long, please.'

Laura found the right nail and dropped it into his gloved palm. 'So, have you decided who is going to benefit from this fixed fence?' she asked. 'Has *Running Livestock For Dummies* got some sort of close-your-eyes-and-point game included?'

'Goats,' Ryan said, taking a nail between his teeth and banging it into a new paling. 'I picked them out at the Minbah market.'

'Goats?' Laura repeated, carefully removing her gaze from the muscles in his tanned forearm, which clenched with every hit. 'Not horses? Not cattle? Not something more overtly…manly?'

Ryan's eyes narrowed as he kept his focus on the nail between his gloved fingers, but his grin only broadened.

It seemed the guy was perfectly secure in his own manliness. More was the pity, because Laura was becoming more and more certain of it herself.

'So what sort of...*goats* did you have in mind?'

'Angora,' he said, with no small amount of pride in his voice.

'What do you know about Angora goats?'

His grin eased into a comfortable smile. 'About as much as I know about cattle or horses.' His bright blue gaze shot her way, creating a ball of fire in her stomach. Laura bit her lip. 'I have a mother and two sisters who can't get enough of Angora,' he said, in between hammer hits. 'I know there is a huge demand for natural fabrics on the Australian fashion scene, and that there is a huge demand for Australian fashion overseas. I know that I can run a small flock on my own, with hired help only at shearing time, and I know that I already have wool buyers lined up across the country and throughout Asia.'

Laura dared not open her mouth for fear that she would come up with nothing more insightful than *duh*. Ryan's growing smile showed that he knew it too.

'So what do you reckon, Ms Somervale? Will I be a farmer yet?'

She felt him getting comfortable, loose-limbed, as if he was born to lean on that fence, and she felt her own need to kick him right out of that comfort zone and back to his side of the fence. Gathering her wits, she pierced him with her fiercest glare and said, 'Nah.'

He shot her a quick glance from the shade of his cap before changing the subject. 'So, why didn't you tell me that you had your eyes on Kardinyarr for yourself?'

Surprised completely, Laura swore beneath her breath.

'Bloody Jill Tucker! Jill told you, right? She can't keep her nose out of this, can she?'

'Out of what?'

'Out of my business,' she said, fudging over the specifics somewhat. 'I never really thought it would ever happen. It was a pipedream, really. Some girls want to be a rock star…'

'You wanted this house and land,' he finished.

'Don't panic. I have no plans to poison your water tanks or knock down your fences in the middle of the night. Unlike *some people*, I am somewhat used to my plans not working out the way I hope they will. It pays to be philosophical about these things.'

'*Some people* being me, right? You think I am used to things working out exactly as *I* planned? As it turns out, Miss Smarty Pants, I do know what it feels like to be told no. And it's not that easy to move on.'

There was something hard in his voice that had her wondering who had denied him. A business associate? A woman? Will? It was Will. That was why he was angry with him. Because if Will had said yes to going to Paris he would not have been walking through the long grass by the gully, he would not have disturbed the deadly brown snake, and he would still have been around today…

She was suddenly aware of how close they were standing. Had she shifted closer to him or he to her? The arm's width distance was now less than a foot. She could feel warmth streaming from his body. She looked up at the stars. *When had they arrived?* she wondered, realising it had fallen dark.

'I have ignored my own rule long enough,' she said. 'Chloe isn't within shouting distance. I had better go. Are you all right for dinner?'

Ryan held a hand to his stomach. 'Thanks to your welcome wagon, I was given six—yes, *six*—pot-roasts today. I will be fine for dinner for the next month.'

'Excellent.' She shot him a quick salute before backing away from his enveloping warmth. 'Goodnight, Ryan.'

'Goodnight, Laura.'

Ryan let out a long slow breath as Laura disappeared within the shadows leading up the drive.

'What are you doing, Gasper?' he asked himself aloud. 'You are asking for trouble, that's what you are doing.'

He reached into the back pocket of his jeans and found Laura's letter. He had kept it on him since the day he'd found it. As first it had been as though if he let it go he would lose the last tenuous link to his brother. But now, the more real the woman in the letter became, the reason for keeping the letter close had changed.

He brought the paper to his lips and imagined he caught a wafting scent. But there was nothing there—only the memory of a woman who smelled so sweet, as though covered in a permanent layer of sugar from her cooking, so sweet it made him ache.

He tucked the letter back into his pocket. The letter that had made him come all the way out to Kardinyarr. And it wasn't just about the information within; it was about the words, the passion, the hope, the wonder—and the woman who had written them.

So what if he had bought the house his brother had loved? That did not give him any right over the woman as well. He was a guy who'd lived out of a suitcase all his life. He was a guy who had told his younger brother to live as he lived, finding companionship wherever he laid his hat, not wanting or needing it to last longer than the weeks or months he stayed in one city. So what right did such a guy have to admire, to want, to long for a woman like Laura?

The laughable thing was that before he had even come, before he had even laid eyes on either of them, he had already been intrigued to distraction by the place—and by the woman. Now that he was getting to know them both, he knew that his imaginings had not even come close to how extraordinary they both were.

Ryan threw his hammer into his shiny new toolbox, grabbed the box, and stormed back to the big house, where the impassive pleasures of fine new furniture and a freezer full of pot-roasts awaited him.

Laura managed to keep out of Ryan's way over the next couple of days. After dropping Chloe at school, she worked her regular part-time shifts at the local post office. Her nights were also full, with Tammy's birthday party one night, and her own *Pirates of Penzance* rehearsal another. So she could fortunately keep Chloe's time with her new champion to a minimum as well.

The peculiar thing was, every time she sneaked her tired little girl home after dark, and she came upon the lit windows of Kardinyarr House, Laura felt joy. She knew it was because every night the windows remained lit was another night Ryan Gasper had lasted. Having a neighbour was enormously comforting. Having him as a neighbour meant that her comfort came with an unpredictable edge.

One evening she found a parcel wrapped in newspaper and string on her welcome mat. She unwrapped the package to find her father's worn, battle-scarred suede gloves. The note with them read: *Symmetry be damned. Keep these safe. R.* The next morning, on the way to dropping Chloe at school, she had left a fresh batch of mini-mince pies on his doorstep, in thanks.

By Friday mid-morning, she had shuttled Chloe to school, cleaned the house, and hung the washing. So by the time Ryan's goats arrived, Laura was crazy with cabin fever. She was used to walking the hills and valleys of her neighbour's farm on a daily basis, and since he had come along she had been stuck in the house, pottering, cooking, and thinking herself in never-ending circles.

She peered out of the kitchen window as the livestock truck trundled up the drive. When it rounded the side of the house she couldn't see any more without leaning herself bodily out of the open window. So she grabbed her gardening gloves and a small spade and hustled outside, where she found an excellent vantage point atop an old fruit crate by the huge lemon tree at the edge of her property.

Her mouth fell agape when she caught a glimpse of Ryan's flock. Not one to start with seeds planted in the ground, he had acquired a seriously healthy, fully-grown herd, which would produce an ample yield of wool. From the looks of it, three of the females were pregnant. Nothing like serious start-up money to get a farm turning a dollar.

Once her curved-up T-shirt was overbrimming with lemons, she ran inside and set to work.

Ryan looked up from gazing at his flock to find Laura striding towards him. He had been expecting her the moment the truck arrived, and wondered what had taken so long.

Rather than her usual sun dresses, she wore faded jeans, moulded tight to her lean curves, and a pale yellow fitted T-shirt. Her curls were tied back into a high-swinging ponytail, again with one of Chloe's pink shoe-laces. The knees of her pants were smeared with dirt and grass stains, and her cheeks were pink from the sun. Her eyes had faint remnants of eyeliner smudged around the edge, making Ryan think she must have had another *Pirates of Penzance* rehearsal the night before. It also made him think how unfairly sexy smudged eyeliner could be on a woman. She looked healthy as sunlight, farm-fed and golden.

'Howdy, ma'am,' Ryan said with a friendly neighbourhood smile when she arrived, doing his best to cover up the fact that she had him entirely unhinged. 'What you got there?'

She lifted a Thermos by way of hello. 'Lemonade. It's a scorcher today, and I thought you could use some.' She rested the Thermos on the railing and poured him a glass. The chilled drink created instant condensation on the outside of the aluminium cup.

He licked his lips as he held out a hand, but looked at her through narrowed eyes. 'Is it homemade?'

She tilted her pretty head to one side. 'Naturally. And using my own lemons.'

'Ms Somervale, I think that they are in fact *my* lemons. The tree trunk is on my side of the fence.'

She glared over at the tree in between their yards. 'You know what?' she said, 'I think you might be right.' Then, easy as you please, she lifted the aluminium cup to her own lips, gulped down the lemonade, then screwed the cap back onto the Thermos without offering him a drop.

'Tease,' Ryan said with a grin, though the clear cool sheen to her lips and the near scent of lemon on her breath tormented him in more ways than one.

'So how's it all going?' she asked, mirroring his stance and lifting one foot onto the bottom rail of the fence, leaning her forearms along the top rail, pulling her jeans tight across her backside.

'Excellent,' Ryan said, unable to hide the longing in his voice.

Laura's eyes narrowed a fraction before flickering over to the placid flock of snowy goats, already attacking the low-hanging leaves of a nearby eucalypt. 'They're precious,' she said.

Their big droopy ears, along with the soft, curling fleece flopping over their eyes and the appearance of a constant smile on their mouths, did give them a sweet, dopey expression. However, Ryan decided to ignore her emasculating jibe.

'They look hot, too,' she said. 'Maybe they would like some lemonade.'

She stepped up on the fence as though she was going to jump over and join them, but Ryan grabbed a hold of her belt loop and tugged her back to the ground. He pulled his hand away before he gave in to any further temptation to touch the smooth line of skin peeking out above the top of her jeans. She kept her eyes on the flock, but he could tell she was grinning from ear to ear.

'They'll be shorn by the end of the month,' he told her, sticking with the conversation topic though his thoughts were on anything but. 'If I don't get to them soon they'll naturally shed, and I'll lose this half-year's fleece. But right now I'm just letting them get used to the place.'

'They'll love it here.'

'I hope so. I paid a mint to an independent breeder for those three females, and they are ready to drop their kids. Then, come autumn I'll stick my top buck in a field with the dozen other mature breeding females and I'll let him have his way with them.'

'How nice for him.'

That earned her a sideways grin. 'They don't seem too upset about it,' he promised. 'If you watch them long enough you'll find the gals are lining up already. He's a stud. Literally.'

'Of course he is. I wouldn't have expected any less from you.' Laura stumbled over her *faux pas*. 'From you…in your choice of stud…goat. Oh, you know what I mean!' She tried to glare at him, but couldn't pull it off with her ruby-red cheeks.

'I know just what you mean,' he agreed, deciding to give her a break. 'Now, local girl, tell me it's going to rain, and soon.'

'It's going to rain and soon,' she echoed, deadpan.

'Excellent. So I guess I should cancel my order for water to be delivered to fill up all my tanks?'

'I wouldn't go that far.'

'Mmm. I wouldn't like to have to do it again every month. It would really cut into my profit margins.' He sensed her glancing his way.

'Wow,' she said. 'You *look* like a real farmer, and now you're starting to *sound* like a real farmer.'

An instant grin stretched across his face. 'The minute I start to smell like a real farmer, you'll let me know?'

'I'll be letting the whole town know.'

He laughed, the sentiment swelling inside of him and radiating warmth to his fingers and toes. In the couple of days out of her company he had almost managed to convince himself he had been imagining the extent of the sparks between them. But now he could almost see the buzz in the air. The energy made him feel as if he could run the perimeter of the property without losing breath.

'I think I am trying to tell you that it's not as easy as looking the part,' Laura said, unexpectedly serious. 'A lot of people try it and simply can't handle the life. If it doesn't work out, and you do leave, don't feel bad.'

She glanced up at him as though gauging his reaction.

'Laura, I know you want the house for yourself, but that is a tad transparent.' He had meant to be joking, but she swallowed in response, hard.

'When I want to be transparent, Ryan, you'll know it,' she said. 'I'm just saying if it all turns bad, and you decide to leave us, you shouldn't feel like a big fat loser.'

He watched for her reaction, and she didn't laugh it off as he'd expected. No, there was more than teasing going on behind her golden eyes.

'And you would be there to buy me out, I assume?'

She flicked her ponytail and lifted her fine chin a fraction. 'Of course I'd get first dibs. So you'd better tell me the minute you're ready to give the place up.'

What was going on? This time she wasn't baiting him. The only way that made sense was if she was actually troubled by the thought of his leaving. 'Laura, if I ever leave this place, you will be the first to know.'

She smiled her thanks, but it was a feeble effort, not even remotely reaching her eyes.

'Now, tell me, neighbour,' he said, deciding to herd the conversation in the opposite direction, to see what else she might give away. 'Since you are obviously so taken by the look, sound, and scent of farm boys, is there some local with his eye on you?'

'Oh, I'm sure there are dozens—hundreds, even.' Her words were thick with sarcasm. She smiled up at him, but there was a question behind the smile. A question Ryan had no intention of answering then and there.

'You mean that the folk in town didn't spill all the gory details about my social life the day you arrived?' she asked.

Ryan held her gaze. 'In fact, no. So why don't you tell me? Is there no big, hunky, overtly manly cow wrangler hoping to become Mr Laura Somervale?'

Her cheeks grew a pretty pale pink and her grin grew disarmingly crooked. 'Nah. Who has the time?'

'Surely there are plenty of local social events at which to, well, socialise?'

'I make my living catering, Ryan. At any local event I am always the one in the apron, with the sweat pouring down my cheeks, as I do the rounds with plates of hot hors d'oeuvres. I hardly make the most beguiling picture.'

'Oh, I don't know,' he said. 'Most guys would do well to find a woman who spends most of her day chained to the kitchen sink. The whole Fifties housewife thing can be a real turn-on.'

This time her glare was full-power. Much better.

'Not to me, of course.' He held a fist in the air. 'Go Women's Lib!'

'Oaf!' she said, and then began running a finger around and around the top of a nail in the fence. 'So, how about you? Is there an exotic yet understanding girlfriend awaiting you in some fabulous overseas locale?'

'Dozens. Hundreds, even,' he said, echoing her own wry retort.

'Really?' She watched him carefully, actually believing that *he* might be telling the truth. Did she really see him as some sort of Lothario? He didn't know whether to be put out or utterly flattered.

'Nah,' he said. 'Who has the time?'

She nodded, and this time her grin was real. Real and utterly arousing. He thought of the long line of beautiful women he *had* met and known in his working life. Elegant Parisians. Enchanting Florentines. Enterprising New Yorkers. Educated, clever, charming women, the lot of them. But none of them, not a single one, had made him feel the desire to decelerate. Not one had had such a deep love of their homeland that simply by being around them he'd felt it too. And not one had made him buy a house, on a farm, miles from a capital city or a members-only club, to instead spend his time with smelly goats and even smellier goat sellers. But this one had done all that and more.

Laura looked out into the field, where the trees dappled sunlight upon the patchy, dusty ground. The lemonade in her hands was beginning to feel slippery in her hot palms. As slippery as their conversation had become.

What was she doing, talking to him about prospective lovers? She had succeeded in keeping him at arm's length these last few days, from her and from Chloe. And within a millisecond of being within his vicinity she'd become a woolly-headed muddle.

She sensed Ryan watching her. She did *not* want to know what he was thinking, and had to bite her tongue to stop herself from asking. *She* was thinking that she very much liked the realisation that the dirt of the land was finding a way into the creases by his eyes, into the soles of his shoes, and into his heart.

He raised one dark eyebrow, smiled, and lifted his hand to shield her eyes from the sun. Laura spun the lid from the Thermos, poured a cup of lemonade, and offered it to him. She watched in mute fascination as he drank it, the column of his unshaven throat working in hard gulps as he downed the cold drink in one breath.

He finished with a satisfied, 'Aah,' wiped his mouth with the back of his arm, and then handed back the empty cup. For all his big-city charm and sophistication, at his core he was simply a fine man.

There was no longer any doubt in her mind. The picture Will had created in her mind all those years before, tempered by getting to know the real, live person, and knowing how much he adored her daughter, had her falling for Ryan Gasper. She was falling like a stone slip-sliding to the bottom of a creek, slowly, inevitably, desperately, hoping a net would catch her before she fell all the way.

Ryan's brow furrowed and he smiled back at her, his straight, white, perfect teeth shining at her from within his gorgeous face. 'What?' he asked.

Maybe it was time to set a few things straight. If they were going to move one way or the other, forward or backward, to friendship or something else, she had to clear the way—for everyone's sake.

'Can I show you something?' she asked. 'Back at my place?'

He blinked back at her, a grin creasing his handsome face. Her heart skittered and leapt in her chest at the awareness of what he was thinking. Yep. It was past time she cleared the way.

'It's about Will,' she said, and was grateful when all temptation cleared from his eyes in an instant.

'Of course it is,' he said. She sensed his hesitation and she understood it. There was unfinished business between Ryan and his brother. She had thought so back then and she knew so now. She sensed it in the stiffness of Ryan's shoulders, in the tension in his voice, in the subtle torment in his steady blue eyes whenever Will's name was mentioned.

She wiped a damp hand on her jeans and held it out for him. 'Come on, Cowboy. It's time.'

He reached out and clasped his hand in hers. His large, warm hand was already lightly callused from the beginnings of the first lot of hard labour he had probably ever done in his life. A slow, steady new warmth swept up her arm, and she knew she was doing the right thing.

She headed towards the house, he followed, and she didn't let go. She led him inside, dodged Chloe's dirty shoes and the obstacle course of furniture, and made her way down the hall.

When they reached her bedroom doorway, Laura baulked. Had she made the bed? Yes, the floral comforter was neatly pulled back in place. Had she put her nightie and underpants in the laundry? Thank goodness, yes! She had hardly been expecting visitors when she'd readied herself. And never in a million years would she have expected this particular visitor.

She tugged. 'Go sit.'

Once Ryan was sitting on the edge of her bed, Laura got down on all fours on the floor, shimmied under the bed and pulled out an old shoebox. Once she had blinked the dust out of her eyes, and removed a piece of lint from her lower lip, she sat on the floor, one foot tucked beneath her, the other leg spread out sideways, the shoebox clutched between her hands.

'I kept all sorts of odd bits and pieces,' she explained. 'Will's things. For Chloe. One day, when the time is right, I want to have something real, something concrete, to connect her to her dad.'

'In case we never showed up,' Ryan finished for her,

and Laura's heart contracted at the regretful twinge in his voice. 'Laura, you don't have to do this.'

'Yes, I do.' She had to, for him. He needed this. He might not know it, but the big strong man perched on the end of her neat bed needed to hear this. It was obvious to her that before he could really move on Ryan needed to know everything that had happened to Will while at Kardinyarr. Until then he was marking time. Entangled in the past. She only hoped she would be able to set him free, help him get past his misplaced anger towards Will, as Will had helped her get past hers towards her father. If Ryan weren't so embroiled in her plan, she knew he would appreciate the symmetry too.

Her hands shook as she pulled away the lid to reveal a neat pile of folded newspaper clippings, letters and knick-knacks—things she had not laid eyes on in years. She reached in and pulled the top one out. It was a clipping about the upcoming World Economic Summit in Paris, several years before. She passed it to Ryan and he took it, his eyes scanning the page until he found the one line about halfway down the page mentioning that, among the special guest speakers, top Australian economist Ryan Gasper would attend.

'He always bought the Melbourne newspapers just in case you might be mentioned in them. There's a couple of dozen more just like it in here.'

'How did you two first meet?' he asked, ignoring her statement as he seemed to stare right through the page.

'I was eighteen when my dad passed away. Within a week Will had taken out a month-by-month lease on Kardinyarr. He came strolling up the drive one day with nothing more than a lazy smile and a backpack.'

Laura shuffled and leant back against the bed, her knees tucked up against her chest, Ryan's feet resting side by side on the floor beside her. When he didn't say anything, she continued.

'From the second we met we hit it off. I needed to talk and he was happy to listen. He needed time to sort out his head, and the peace and quiet around here gave him that. He told me that my pies would be my fortune, and I believed him. I told him that so long as he followed his heart he would be fine, and he believed me. It was as though the fates had landed us together in that brief moment in our lives for a reason.'

And that was all we were, Laura thought. *Two lonely kids reaching out for emotional comfort through physical means.* She only hoped Ryan could see what she was trying to tell him without her having to say it aloud.

Ryan placed the old newspaper clipping carefully on the bed. 'He loved you, Laura,' he said, and it wasn't a question.

She shook her head, her curls making a shuffling noise against the bed sheets. 'No, not in the way that you think. I think in the end he put me on a pedestal, the same way he did you.'

A brief glance flickered her way.

'The way he spoke about you…' she continued. 'He worshipped you, Ryan. I think half of him thought he ought to be more like you—to work hard, to live big. But the other half wanted nothing more than to lie back on a trampoline and stare at the stars for the rest of his life. I often wonder if that's what he saw in me: if I was the girl least likely to turn his big brother's head, so he used me as the ultimate rebellion.'

She kept her head down as she played with the corner of an old letter in the shoebox, waiting in breathless silence for his reaction. But the last thing she'd expected him to do was reach out and run a hand over her hair.

'Don't do that to yourself, sweetheart,' he insisted, his voice raw with emotion. 'Maybe in the beginning he came all the way out here purposely walking steps I had never taken, but don't you *ever* think that *you* could be something so trivial as somebody else's insurrection.'

'It was just a fleeting thought,' she said. One that had crept up on her repeatedly over the years.

He didn't stop caressing her hair, and she didn't pull away. He tucked one stray curl after another into his palm, running them through his work-roughened fingers. Her eyes drifted closed as she allowed herself the decadent pleasure of revelling in Ryan's deft touch.

But there was more to say. 'That last week,' she said, her voice sounding softer, further away, almost like a purr, 'you invited him to join you in Paris.'

'I did.' His voice reverberated through his fingers, creating tingles in her scalp.

'I've figured out, from the things you have said, that you didn't know…he was planning to go.'

'He what?' Ryan's fingers stopped their digression through Laura's curls.

This was it. She sucked in a deep breath, a cool column of air chilling her from the inside out. 'That morning,' she said, referring to Will's last day, 'he was taking a final walk around the property to say his goodbyes.'

'Goodbyes?'

'He had told me he was leaving. He had told me that he'd thought about it and that he wanted to join you in Paris after all.'

Ryan leant forward, hiding his face in his open palms. She fought the urge to wrap her arms about his legs and hug away the hurt.

'Will…he told me about you,' Ryan said at long last, pulling one hand from his face to reach out to her. 'He told me he had met you. *I* told him to let you go, to move on, to spread his wings before he even thought about settling down. That's why I wanted him in Paris. To take him away from you. Laura, sweetheart, I am so sorry. It was all my fault.'

She spun on the floor to face him and his hand slipped to his side. 'No, but don't you see? I agreed that he needed to experience life. He was still so young at heart, and with such a young soul. I told him to try and see it your way, to give you a chance before he could ever really know if he wanted to take a different path in life from yours. He was coming to Paris, Ryan, because I asked him to leave.'

CHAPTER SEVEN

RYAN stared at Laura, assimilating her bombshell. *She* had asked Will to leave. He felt as if he was on the verge of something—a breakthrough or a breakdown. Either way, he had to see her tale through to its very end.

'Did you love him, Laura? Did you love my brother?' His heart slammed against his ribs as he awaited her answer. If she told him yes, that despite everything she'd loved Will, then that would be that. He would leave well enough alone. But if in fact he had been wrong all along…

'I cared for him deeply,' she said, heeding her words. 'He helped me through the most rotten time of my life. But we were so young. Kids, really. Both alone and lonely. I think we both found a great deal of solace in each other's arms. But no, Ryan, I was never *in love* with him.'

With that, she spun about onto her knees and leant her lovely face into his palm. 'Ryan, please don't hate me. When he died, I almost fell apart. Two people so dear to me gone in such a short time—I felt like I'd never find my feet again. The day after Will died Jill found me dropped over the bath, too worn out to move. She took me to see Dr Gabriel in town, and that's when I found out I was four weeks pregnant. I didn't have the luxury to wallow, or to fade away. Having someone else to care for made me grow up quick-smart. And then you came along and made me remember…made me wonder if I treated him badly.'

Ryan snapped out of his trance. He cupped his hand beneath her dainty chin, making sure she was looking him in the eye as he spoke. 'Laura, sweetheart, you couldn't treat someone badly if you tried. If you had lessons. If you had someone coaching you on how to do it.'

'I need to know that I haven't hurt your feelings in telling you all this,' she said. 'It just felt like the right thing to do. To clear the air. So that we both know where we stand. I feel like we have forged a…friendship these last days, and I need to be honest with my friends.'

She amazed him. Talk about being a grown-up. He didn't know if he had it in him to be as forthright and honest as she was being right then. He knew he didn't have half her strength, unable as he was to tell her the extent of the feelings he had been fighting against for days.

Ryan ran his thumb over the softness of her cheek, and he knew he had wanted to touch her like this since the moment he'd laid eyes on her. He tucked his hand behind her neck, deep into the soft haven of her curls, making sure he held her eye contact the whole way.

'My turn to set some things straight,' he said, his throat so tight he felt as though he was swallowing razorblades. 'I don't think Will chose you because you were the least likely to turn my head, Laura. I think he knew how much I would admire your spirit, how readily I would react to your artless beauty, and even how much I would be fascinated by the charming cadence of your speech.'

She didn't break eye contact once. Amazing. 'You know that first day,' she said, 'when you wandered up onto my lawn in your new jeans and shiny boots? I thought you were pretty hot stuff too.'

Ryan couldn't stop the charmed laugh that escaped his throat. He reached out, tucking a stray ringlet back within the rage of curls at her neck. 'Chloe spilled the beans on that one already.'

'Why am I not surprised?' she said, her eyes bright and guileless. 'But you can't blame me. I'm a single mother, living all alone in the middle of nowhere. What was I supposed to think?'

He laughed aloud, the pleasure of it creating great relaxing waves down his length. 'I have never met anyone like you before, Laura. You are fearless.'

She shook her head. 'I am so scared right now I can barely catch my breath.'

'You? Scared? I don't believe it.'

'Believe it.'

The hitch in her voice drew his gaze from the silky softness of her curls back to her glittering eyes. And only then did he see it. Beneath the cheeky flare, beneath the frisky smile, was the slow-burning flame of an impossible attraction. Feelings she could no longer hide even though she knew she must. Feelings for him.

And what made it even worse was that he knew exactly how she felt. Affected beyond reason, he delved his hand deeper, sinking sweetly until it rested behind her warm neck. Then, as though it was the most natural thing in the world to do, he kissed her.

After the briefest moment of hesitation, Laura melted completely beneath him. Her soft groan was smothered as her smooth, warm lips melded perfectly against his. Her hand reached into the hair at his neck and she pulled herself up onto her knees, leaning her length against him, pressing her breasts against his chest, sliding her spare arm tight about his torso.

The immediacy of her need blinded him to all reason, and Ryan was soon swept from diffident and discovering into scorching and intense. Fire sparks danced behind his eyes as he slipped deeper and deeper under Laura's dazzling wave of explosive passion. His stomach muscles ached as he struggled to stem his powerful appetite.

On a dull groan, he wrapped her up tighter in his arms. One hand slipped straight beneath the cotton T-shirt to stroke the writhing velvet heat of the skin on her back, the other hand diving beneath the belt of her soft jeans, and the sensation as he felt the rounded bump of the top of her buttocks sent him spiralling into rapture.

Aeons later Laura came up for breath, and at the sudden wisp of cool air against his hot mouth Ryan saw himself clearly. What the hell was he doing? Taking advantage of her in a deeply sensitive moment, that was what!

He disentangled his arms from about her exquisite body and shot to his feet. 'I'm sorry. I don't know why—I shouldn't have— Damn it!'

'Ryan, really, it's okay,' Laura said, watching him with wide eyes. She hadn't pulled away because it had felt wrong! Though every nerve in her entire being had sprung to life, though as his warm lips had brushed against hers her whole body had jolted with electricity, though she had not been able to feel the ground beneath her knees, or even the clothes on her back, she had never felt more unwavering, more complete, more sure. But as Ryan paced back and forth, running ravaging fingers through his hair, it was obvious he did not feel the same way.

Laura swallowed down her disappointment. 'Ryan,

stop. Please. We are both trying our best to fudge our way through a difficult situation here. Neither of us really knows what we are doing and we only have each other to lean on. Emotions are high. It's only natural that something like that would occur.'

And the fact that I have imagined that kiss, dreamed of how your lips would feel, sure doesn't help, she thought. Maybe she should just tell him that she wanted it too. Perhaps it would make it easier for him if he only knew how attracted to him she was. Still, if he hadn't figured it out from her consuming reaction to his kiss…

This was more than chemistry. There had been plenty of opportunities for her to pursue relationships since Will. Some nice men had taken her on dates and whispered sweet nothings in her ear, but she had always been the one to pull away before she got too close.

So why didn't she just put up that wall—that big, hard, tough I-am-a-mother-and-nothing-else-is-as-important-as-that wall—and be done with it? Because she knew that some things were just as important as being a good mother. When Ryan looked at her he made her feel utterly female. Not like a cook, or a mother, or a daughter. But like a woman. And she was addicted. She wanted more.

But the problem was, after all this effort at clearing the air, she still had no idea where *he* stood. He was taken with her, that she knew. But how much? Enough for him to push through any mental barrier in order to have her?

'Maybe you should add this letter to the collection.' Laura looked up to find Ryan holding out the letter she had written to his family all those years before. She'd thought he had brought it with him as evidence to prove he was who he said he was. But he still had it on him—it seemed—at all times.

'I can't take that.'

'Why not?' he asked on a heavy sigh. His chest still heaved as he tried to bring his breathing back to a normal pace.

'Because I try very hard not to remember writing the thing. I was young. Upset. Hormonal. Alone.'

'You were wonderful. If Chloe is going to have these precious mementos of her father, I think she needs to see this as well. To see what a strong, amazing, generous, loving woman her mother is.'

If you think I am all those things, why did you pull away from my kiss as though you had been burned?

'Please. I am hardly any of those things. Amazing, sure. But the rest—I don't think so,' she said, trying for sassy.

Ryan reached out and took her hands, drawing her to her feet. She stopped babbling and gazed into his impassioned blue eyes. 'Joke all you want, Laura, but I am being utterly serious here. This letter…I have never read anything like it. Most people would not have the guts to present such a gift of knowledge to those who could take everything away from them. You didn't know us at all, and if Will told you anything, we must have seemed the most terrifying family on the planet.'

'When your sister played the violin at his funeral…I had never heard anything like it,' Laura admitted. 'I was pretty terrified that you guys had the means and the power to take Chloe away from me.'

'Yet you sent the letter anyway?'

She shrugged. 'Of course. I knew it wasn't about me. I would fight. I would survive. It was about Chloe. You are her family too. And I…I am glad you have found us. Finally.'

'Finally,' he repeated, and by the stormy look in Ryan's eyes Laura was sure he was about to pull her into his arms and kiss the breath from her lungs once more.

But he took a decided step away and she all but stumbled.

'I think it's time I headed home,' he said, his voice cool and distant. 'I want to spend some time with the goats to make sure they're settled. Introduce them to their water troughs and the dry shed and such.'

'Oh, okay.' Her whole body went slowly numb as she followed Ryan to her front door. She had been so hell-bent on helping Ryan out of his blue funk that she had instead danced him blindly right into another. It seemed she had two left feet, as well as a terrible singing voice.

Ryan bestowed upon her a strange half-smile before walking from her door, leaving her feeling as if she had gone ten rounds in a heavyweight fight. And she had no idea if she had won or lost.

Ryan couldn't sleep. The heat had reached the high thirties again that day, but the famously changeable regional temperature had dropped to half that in the last two hours. A change was coming through. He sat on the back veranda, watching the dark, cloud-filled sky, wishing for rain and reliving his startling afternoon with Laura.

The guilt that had plagued him for so many years no longer felt so crushing. Through Laura's optimistic eyes he even felt as though he understood his little brother more. Will had been a kid, exploring his own path, and doing pretty well in his search. Will had found a woman of value, he had supported her and learnt from her. Somehow, that one idea alone brought more comfort than he had felt in years. Laura had given him that, and Ryan saw, looking back, that that had been her intention the whole time.

But as to *his* relationship with Laura? He was more confused about that than ever. Had she shown him the shoebox as a way to get him to back off? To show him that her life was complicated enough as it was? Or had she been telling him that her heart was free? Her spectacular reaction to his kiss suggested it was the latter.

By two o'clock in the morning he needed a good excuse to get away from the house. He had barely lived in the place long enough to accumulate much rubbish, but he threw a light Mackintosh over his T-shirt, took his one bag of trash out to his big plastic wheelie bin, and set off. By the time he had rolled the bin the hundred metres to the front gate it had begun to pour—big, hard, fat splashes of rain.

It was too far to run for cover, and the only nearby shade was a tree by Laura's dam. But an obese cow already held her ground there, and he wasn't sure she would appreciate his company. So, instead, he just gave in to the downpour. He tipped his head back and drank in the cool drops. Heavenly drops which would hopefully fill his tanks, would fill his water troughs over the hill and give his gorgeous goats a fighting chance.

The goats must have heard his bumpy travels, as they were standing, bleating, at the fence when he jogged back up the hill. Of the pregnant goats, two still had great stomachs—but one did not. Some time that day she had dropped her young.

He swore beneath his breath before leaping over the fence. Mabel. The one without the large tummy was the one he had called Mabel. Her mid-section was stretched and flaccid, and she had dried blood below her tail. Even a city boy could tell she was no longer carrying.

'Bloody hell. What have you done, Mabel?'

The goat bleated at him and nudged his hand. According to Doc Larson's instructions, and the how-to book he had finished reading earlier that night, she seemed all right. She was upright, alert, mobile. But what about her kids? Where the heck were they?

Rain slashed across his field of vision. The half-hidden moon lit patches of high grass and missed dark puddles of gathering water. Where would she have dropped? It could be anywhere.

The dry. The front shed!

Ryan rushed through the thrashing rain to the shed halfway up the near hill. Inside, he found a litter of two laid out on a pile of straw. One, though weak, was healthy, pink and bleating. The other was still. Too still.

This was not all about Will any more. It wasn't even about Laura Somervale and her adorable daughter. This was about life and death. In his ridiculous he-man pretence at fitting in he had taken on these strange creatures, and therefore it was up to him to look out for them. If this little one died… He swallowed down the thought. But what to do? What to do?

Mabel had followed him in, and she set about nursing the crying baby, blithely ignoring the still one.

Remembering a mishmash of advice from his book and from the farmers at the Minbah market, he checked that the feed in the shed was still dry for the goats huddled inside. The last thing he needed was to lose his new flock to damp, mouldy feed. He opened up the bale and checked deep inside. It smelt sweet and felt dry. Good news.

Leaning on instinct, he tore off his Mackintosh, whipped off his warm, dry T-shirt, grabbed the still kid, and wrapped it up tight. He pulled the Mac over his head and, with the precious package under his arm, ran through the dark rain, keeping his footing on the slippery ground more through will-power than through clever footwork, until he'd run up the steps and into the warm house. He ran straight to the kitchen and turned on the oven to a low heat.

Unwrapping the little creature on the kitchen table, he lost himself for a moment. There was simply no evidence of life. No swelling breaths. No niggling noises. The poor limp kid was cold as any stone. He carefully slid his hands beneath its torso and placed it on a hand towel, then on a tray in the oven. Leaving the door open, he sat upon the slate floor, cross-legged, and waited.

And waited. And waited. Topless and shivering. But he couldn't leave. Not yet. Not while there was still hope.

His own sneeze startled him several minutes later. And a soft mewling sound in his ear reminded him why he was sitting, soaking wet, on the cold kitchen floor.

The baby goat. It was alive. Eureka!

He turned off the oven and with slow, careful hands brought the goat into his lap. The towel on which the goat lay was warm and crispy, making Ryan realise how cold he really was.

He ran a finger down the little one's back, revelling in the feel of the skin and the muscles moving beneath his touch. He had saved its life. He wanted to run, scream, and wake the neighbours to tell them what he had done. He pictured Chloe's excited laughter at seeing a newborn kid take its first look at life. He pictured Laura's parting smile, careful and unsure. Maybe this would turn it around, bring back the easy camaraderie they had enjoyed before the shoebox had been opened. But it was the middle of the night. He would have to enjoy this moment on his own.

He carefully got to his feet, keeping the kid as steady as possible. He found an old moving box, and tucked her inside with a throw rug while he made a fire. Then he braved the rain again, found Mabel, and gathered a cupful of first milk. Without that, the kid still might not stand a chance. Sitting back beside the kid's makeshift nest, he soaked his finger and let the little one drink the elixir. After five minutes of sipping its way towards a healthy life, the goat shuffled in its makeshift bed, and even tried to stand on wobbly feet.

'Whoa, little one. Settle down. You have the rest of your life to be a grown-up. Now, I'll let you stay in here tonight, but tomorrow you'll have to face the big bad world. No use cosseting you from reality, as then you will never have the chance to grow big and strong.'

Post speech, he sneezed again, and this time he felt it all the way deep into his lungs. More exhausted than he could ever remember being, Ryan grabbed a cushion and another throw rug and curled up on the couch by the makeshift crib. And somehow, on what was one of the most mentally exhausting days of his life, he fell asleep, feeling as though the last of his demons were floating away with his dreams.

Laura let Chimp out for a run in the mud puddles early the next morning. The house next door looked all too quiet. The windows were closed up tight. The back screen door was shut. Ryan's boots were still on the back stoop. Moreover, the goats had gathered about the front shed, as though they too were waiting for the morning to begin. Something wasn't right.

Biting at her bottom lip, she fought the need to check up. Maybe after what had happened between them the day before he'd had a late-night bender and was sleeping off a hangover. What if all her soul-searching had scared him away? What if he had felt pressured by her reaction to his kiss? Maybe he'd decided to do a runner in the middle of the night? That was enough to send Laura sprinting over to Kardinyarr House.

'Knock, knock!' she called out, before slipping inside the unlocked back door. She walked slowly down the Kardinyarr House hallway for the first time since Ryan had moved in. A huge antique mirror had pride of place at the end of the hall. A Tasmanian oak dining setting and a stunning antique credenza filled the dining room perfectly. Stuffed leather sofas, deep red rugs, and a wall full of periodicals and textbooks littered the formal sitting room.

She would have expected all black, white and chrome from a city boy trying to fit his square life into a round country setting. But, no. It looked…beautiful. It looked as a home should. Ryan had a feel for the place. Or perhaps the place had a feel for him.

But right now the house felt eerily quiet. No noises came from the kitchen. No rustle of newspapers or general manly noises could be heard anywhere.

'Ryan?' she called, as she poked her head into the lounge room, but the word faded on her lips at the sight that met her.

Big, burly Ryan Gasper was curled up on an extra-long lounge chair with a tiny newborn goat snuggled into the crook of his bare arm. He was naked, bar a pair of jeans and a throw rug covered him to his shins, big bare feet poking out the end. The remnants of a fire had burned itself out in the grate, so the room was cool.

His usually determined face was peaceful and smooth, his thick dark eyelashes rested against suntanned cheeks, and his mouth lay ever so slightly open as he slept. Oh, what a beautiful man…

Chimp must have followed her inside, as from nowhere he suddenly leapt up onto the couch, his muddy paws landing right on Ryan's stomach.

'Chimp, get down!' Laura whispered, but it was too late.

Ryan jackknifed, and his flailing feet tipped over a bowl of milk which had been sitting on the ground near the couch. 'What?' he cried out, his voice deep and sexy with sleep. 'What's going on?'

He stared at Laura with wild eyes, and she stared back, her hand covering her mouth to stop her laughter. He was hopping about on one foot, trying to keep the milk-splashed foot off the ground. Half his face was creased, red with the geometric pattern of the cushion imprinted on his cheek. He was shirtless, his glorious array of muscles tense as he held on tight to the tiny creature in his arms.

'Ryan, it's Laura.'

Ryan let out a huge sneeze that had Chimp running for cover. 'Why? What's wrong?'

Laura's gaze fell back to Ryan's strong arms. 'Why don't you ask Munchkin there?'

Brow furrowed, Ryan's head tipped downwards, and then remembrance of what must have been one strange night dawned on his face. 'She's alive,' he said, his voice almost a whisper. He ran a large finger delicately down the kid's soft back.

Laura swallowed. Hard. The look in Ryan's eyes was

enough to have her melt on the spot. It was a goat, for goodness' sake! Livestock. A means towards profit maximisation. Not anything to goo and gah about! But there was just something about a grown man acting with such tenderness that got her where it mattered.

'And she's hungry,' she added, doing all she could to crack the delicate mood before she burst into tears or threw herself into his arms. 'How many young do you have?'

But Ryan looked so bewildered Laura stepped in further. 'Would you like my help to find out if there are any others?'

A smile creased his sleep-softened face, and he said, 'I would like that very much.'

'Right. Well. Good. Fine.' Laura struggled to remember what he would like very much as the tone in his voice was rather more provocative than she had anticipated.

But then the kid bleated, and Laura remembered. The livestock. A born-and-bred farm girl, animals she could cope with. She was still having trouble with big, gorgeous, half-naked men she had kissed until she'd all but passed out. 'Great,' she said, clapping her hands with vigour. 'It's a little cooler out today, so you'd better put on something warm before following me.'

Ryan looked around for somewhere to put the kid. *Put it on the floor!* Laura thought, but he had such a proprietary stance she knew he wouldn't bear such a suggestion.

'Oh, just give the thing to me!' she said, reaching out and cradling the infant in her arms.

Ryan padded off on bare feet, scratching his head as he wandered to his bedroom. The goat looked up at

Laura with liquid eyes. Shaking her head, she tucked her fingers beneath its soft chin and looked right back.

'Ooh, you know just how to bat those lashes, don't you, Munchkin? You've got that big galoot right where you want him. Maybe you could teach me a trick or two.'

An hour later, Laura and Ryan had checked on the other newborns. Three more had dropped through the night, and all were well. It took some time for Laura to encourage Mabel to take little Munchkin on the teat, for by that stage she smelled more like Ryan than like goat.

'You have to be more careful with that next time. You're just lucky that Mabel is a big softy. Munchkin could very well have been rejected.'

Ryan shrugged. 'So—then I would have fed her, and raised her as an indoor goat.'

Sitting there, watching the future of his farm growing before his eyes, he looked as happy as a pig in mud. A smile lay easily on his mouth, and his gaze skimmed over his flock. Laura fought the urge to pull a strand of hay from his hair. Heck, it looked so adorable in there, maybe she'd never tell him.

'Me and Munchkin against the world,' he continued. 'I would take her with me in the car whenever I went into town.'

She stared at him. The guy had gone cuckoo. Overnight he had shed his inhibitions and become…happy. She had heard him sneeze a couple of times; perhaps he was delirious with fever.

'The townsfolk would look at us as we drove past,' he continued, 'shaking their heads, but smiling all the while. "There goes Munchkin with that silly goat," they would say.'

And then Laura knew he was pulling her leg. She

wasn't usually so gullible, but this man just knew how to push her buttons, ring her bells, and make her tremble… She shot to her feet. 'Well, it seems you're all sorted now. You and your goats seem happy enough, so I'll leave you to it.'

Ryan scrambled to his feet and ran his palms down the sides of his jeans. 'You don't want to come in for breakfast?'

'Not today.'

'Oh.' His disappointment was palpable—and tempting. 'But Chloe doesn't have school today, right? Why don't you both come over? This time I can cook for you.'

First he made her coffee, and now he wanted to cook her breakfast. Help! 'Not today. Chloe didn't have a good night last night; we've been up with a bad cough. I'd rather keep the excitement level at a low today. For her. Her excitement level.'

And mine, she thought. Even if Chloe hadn't had a bad night, Laura wouldn't have slept a wink as it was. She had been up most of the night, sitting on the window-seat in her room, wrapped in her comforter, thinking of the future. No matter how many times she played it out in her mind, when she thought about where they would all be in six months' time, when winter set in and living on the land was not so easy to love, for the life of her she could not imagine Ryan still living next door. Seeing him with Munchkin in his arms hadn't changed that. So no more mooning over him. No more falling under the spell of his relentless blue gaze. And definitely no more kissing! Her head was still kind of fuzzy from exhaustion, and she wasn't sure she could handle Ryan in such an endearing mood.

'Another time,' she said, hoping she could avoid the invitation for ever. She called to Chimp, who was busy trying to round up the goats, who were blithely ignoring him, and went home.

CHAPTER EIGHT

THE next morning, Laura found Chimp hiding behind her mother's antique chaise-longue.

'It is a beautiful warm bath that will leave you feeling like a million bucks!' she insisted, as she dragged the dog into her arms. 'I never get the chance to have a hot bath, and here you are, refusing one!'

She set Chimp down in the lukewarm chest-high water in the laundry sink, hitched her old, worn tracksuit pants back up to a discreet level on her hips, and dived into the project at hand. Once he was squeaky clean, Laura put him on a towel on the floor. He instantly shook himself until she ended up with soapy water all down her front. She grabbed a corner of the cotton towel to dry her face, and when Chimp saw his opening he took off.

'Chimp—stay!' Laura called out, but Chimp was conveniently temporarily deafened by the water in his ears.

She took off after him, following the trail of suds through the lounge room and out through the open front door. When she caught up to him Chimp was halfway across the yard and already rolling in a grass-free patch of dirt.

'Why, you little….'

Sensing imminent danger, Chimp raced off again, across the rest of the yard and through the gate, where he knew he was not meant to go without an escort.

'Chimp!' Laura tiptoed across the rocky ground in her bare feet. When she rounded the Japanese maple, she all but ran into Ryan. Her breath caught at the sight of him leaning against her front gate, in jeans and a cable-knit jumper, morning coffee cup in hand, one foot hooked up onto a tree stump.

Chimp stood behind Ryan, using him as a human shield, panting and watching her as though sensing the complete collapse of her authority.

'Hi,' Ryan said, his voice all laid-back gorgeousness that melted her inside and out.

'Hi,' she said back, casually crossing her arms over her wet T-shirt. She saw that his new jeans were fading, they even held a couple of stubborn stains and a tear in one leg. 'Were you waiting here for me?'

He shrugged. 'I knew you'd stick your nose out sooner rather than later. I wanted to see how Chloe was doing today.'

'Much better, thanks. She had a good night. It was probably the sudden change in weather that brought it on. Emergency averted. How's Munchkin?'

He stared at her for a few moments, his blue eyes baffled, and then realisation dawned. 'Oh, the baby goat! She's doing fine.'

'The kid,' Laura corrected.

'Hmm?' he said through a sip of coffee.

'Not baby goat, Ryan. It's called a kid.'

His face broke into a cunning smile. 'You couldn't let that go, could you?'

'I wouldn't want you making a fool of yourself in company.'

'That's rot. You love correcting me. The farm girl putting the city boy in his place. But, as a great man once said "a rose by any other name would smell as sweet".'

She hitched her drooping old pants back to her hips,

and then recrossed her arms over her wet T-shirt. 'I can simply stop jumping in to help altogether, if that's what you want. No more saving you from yourself.'

'Sweetheart, I am counting on you to save me from myself.'

At Ryan's instant about-face, Laura's mouth snapped closed. There was more behind that comment than back-pedalling. More behind his eyes than fun and games. Something had changed in him, but she hadn't a clue what. A very different kind of energy arced between them—an energy completely commanded by the man smiling back at her with a gleam in his eye.

'Speaking of making a fool of myself,' he drawled, 'I heard the Tandarah Mini-golf Championship is on this afternoon.'

Laura blinked.

Ryan blinked right back. 'It's like golf. Only smaller.'

'I know what mini-golf is. I'm just surprised that a big-city fella like you would be interested.'

'I'm more than interested. I plan to win.'

'Please! *I* have won the tournament the last two years, and *I* plan on making it a hat-trick.' As soon as the words were out of her mouth she knew—he had known that all along, and she had just fallen into his trap.

'Great!' he said, the half-smile splitting into a full-on beam, and she had to brace her knees to stop them from collapsing out from under her. 'No point in taking two cars. I'll pick you and Chloe up around eleven?'

'I don't know, Ryan…'

'I thought it was about time that Chloe and I did something social together. With you as chaperon, of course. She's feeling better; you're defending champion. So it's a date.' He backed away down the drive.

'Ryan, you can drive us to Tandarah, but I promise you it won't be a date.'

Unfazed, he shot her a little wave before bounding up onto his veranda and inside Kardinyarr House. This left Chimp without a shield. Laura reached down and grabbed the dirty, wet dog.

'He is just so exasperating!' she yelled to the fluffy white clouds. But they ignored her attempt to convince herself that exasperation was her prime emotion when it came to Ryan Gasper.

Laura had every intention of being dressed, ready and waiting, by Ryan's car by ten minutes to eleven. The less this whole escapade felt like a *date* the better. She had to let Ryan off the hook, move the friendship back towards neighbourly, so that when he had had his fill of getting to know her little girl, when he went back to his jet-setting lifestyle, she would not fall apart again and he wouldn't feel guilty for leaving.

But by ten minutes to eleven she had a towel holding up her damp hair, she could not find her lucky shoes, and Chloe was nowhere to be seen.

'Chloe!' Laura called, with her toothbrush in her mouth. 'Tell me you are ready!'

She stormed to the front door, and pulled up short to find Ryan standing on the other side of the flyscreen. Decked out in casual beige trousers and a navy designer polo shirt, he did things to her equilibrium—even with the softening effect of the mesh in between them.

'You're early!' she accused.

He pulled the door open and invited himself in. 'You're not,' he said. His blue eyes scanned over her makeshift hairdryer with blatant interest.

'Sure I am. I find the towel gives me better balance

when I putt.' His gaze shot to her eyes, so filled with humour that she had to bite her lip to stop from grinning inanely back at him. 'If you think it's an unfair advantage, you could always give me a minute to lose it.'

His gaze flicked up to her turban, then back down again. 'Laura, it wouldn't make a lick of difference. You have all sorts of unfair advantages over the likes of me.'

'Oh,' she said, her voice ridiculously breathy. She could have kicked herself where she stood.

Chloe, barefoot, with her plaits already coming undone, bundled in from outside, with Chimp at her heels.

'Shoes, Chloe!' Laura demanded, stepping away from Ryan's concentrated presence. 'We are going in two minutes.'

'All right, already!' Chloe harrumphed, before skipping into her bedroom.

'Wait here,' she demanded of Ryan, before disappearing down the hall and out of his sight.

Ryan traipsed into the kitchen, where a tray of fresh scones lay cooling on the bench. Strips of crisp hot dough lay like rays of sunshine across the top of each. She couldn't possibly notice if one of them went missing…

Above the humming sound of a real hairdryer, Laura's voice boomed from down the hall. 'Ryan! If those scones look any different when I get out there, you will lose a hand.'

Ryan's fingers snapped back, away from temptation and into his trouser pocket. The woman was good!

When she came back, hair curling softly over her shoulders, Ryan remembered she was more than good. She was stunning.

Hipster denim jeans held up with a wide brown belt and an embellished pink top clung to a flawless arrangement of trim curves. Ryan almost called out in protest when she wrapped a lurid gold button-down shirt over her shoulders, hiding her stunning figure. But then, lest it drag about her knees, she tied the shirt at her waist, and she was delectable again. She grabbed a big cream sunhat and a soft handbag and joined him in the kitchen.

'Nice shirt,' he said, focusing on the only part of her get-up that didn't have him salivating more than he had been over the scones.

She spun on the spot so he could read the writing on the back. It read: *Tandarah Mini-golf Champion*.

'Impressive,' he said. 'Do you get to keep it when you lose today? Or do you have to pass it on to the next champ? That, of course, being me.'

Her eyes narrowed. 'I get to keep it. And today I will add another, the *third* I shall have hanging in my closet.'

'Mmm. Three shiny gold shirts made big enough to fit any self-respecting trucker. You need never go shopping for clothes again.'

'So stay home if the idea of winning one doesn't appeal,' she dared. 'The petrol tank in my car is full.'

He raised a hand to his heart and did his best to look contrite. 'Did you think I was being disparaging? On the contrary. I just think that shirt of yours would fit me a heck of a lot better than it fits you.'

Outwitted, she dropped her arms, searched in her handbag for her house keys and walked past him with her eyes dead ahead. 'Ask me nicely, Cowboy, and I might even let you try it on one day.' She grabbed the tray of scones, along with a small cooler from the fridge, her lean hips swinging saucily as she sauntered away. It was a view he could get used to. Purple pants, tight jeans; the colour didn't seem to make any difference to his libido. But it seemed it was a view he would have to get used to, as she seemed to walk away a heck of a lot more than she walked towards him.

'Chloe, we are leaving!' she yelled, and the little one materialised from goodness knew where, trussed up in overalls, pink sneakers, and with an odd assortment of clips in her hair, which were half falling out already.

'Can we take Chimp?' Chloe asked.

'Not today, possum. Pop him inside, and we'll bring him back a treat, okay?'

Ryan followed the girls out through the front door, silently taking the tray from Laura's hand so she could lock up.

Chloe looked up at him, her eyes squinting in the bright sunlight. 'Are we really going in your car, Ryan?'

'Yep. Is that okay?'

Chloe looked over at his black sports car, which was all but beige with dust. 'Sure,' Chloe said with a shrug. 'Though I do think it's the most ridiculous sort of car to have on a farm.'

Ryan burst into laughter, knowing exactly where the little girl had picked up that opinion.

'Chloe!' Laura chastised her, tucking her daughter behind her as they traipsed towards the car in question. A familiar blush crept up her cheeks.

Ryan crouched down to Chloe's height. He would never get used to her scent—a wonderful mix of strawberries, grass and baby powder. 'So, what sort of car do you think I should have instead?'

'Do I really get to choose?'

'I am happy to listen to your opinions,' he said, covering himself.

'Umm…' she said, poking a finger in her mouth as she thought deeply. She leaned against him and he felt something distinctly paternal swell within him. As if a pact had been made in that instant. He would uphold her instinctive trust to the end of time.

Her face lit up. 'You should get a pink Corvette. Like Barbie's. Tammy got one for her birthday. It's the coolest car ever!'

'Whenever you two are done yabbering,' Laura said from behind them, 'I have a tournament to win. And the jam and cream in that cooler will not last long in this sun.'

Ryan stood and looked over to find Laura watching them from beneath her large floppy sunhat. Her bottom lip had half disappeared between her teeth, as though she was trying to bite back a smile.

'Let's go! I don't want to miss the candyfloss!' Chloe called out, taking his hand in her small, hot, sticky grip.

And, just like that, Laura's smile slipped away; she forcibly broke eye contact and glared at his car. 'Is there even enough space in the back seat of that contraption to fit a child, scones, and a cooler?'

'Well, just think how privileged you should feel in being the one to find out.' Ryan opened up, pushed the seat forward, and helped Chloe scoot into the back seat, then helped her with her seat belt. As she sat back, allowing him to take care of her, again he felt the dawning knowledge that he was mad about this kid. He swallowed hard as he slid the tray of food next to Chloe, wrapping it in its own seat belt as well, which had Chloe giggling.

'Your mum can hardly complain now, can she?' he whispered to her.

'I don't know about that,' Chloe said with a shrug. 'When she wants to, she can always find something to complain about. Like how she always ends up giving Chimp a bath. But I'm too short to reach the tub. And now you're next door she can't hang washing on the line in her underwear.'

'Chloe!' Laura warned her, and Chloe sank back into her seat, head down, hands clasped demurely in her lap.

Ryan pushed the passenger seat back into place, and left only just enough room for Laura to slip past him.

'Don't let me stop you,' he whispered, before she slid into the car.

She looked him in the eye, their faces mere inches apart. 'You think she has a smart mouth? You just try pushing me, Cowboy, and I promise I can tell you some things that will have your city-boy ears turning as red as a Kardinyarr sunset.' And then she was in the car, shuffling her cute backside into his bucket seat, making sure he knew how uncomfortable she was.

Not willing to give in without a fight, Ryan leant into the car and reached across her, his arm resting against her warm torso, pinning her to the back of the seat. 'Do you need help with *your* seat belt?'

She glared at him, but not before moistening her lips with a quick stroke of her pale pink tongue. 'No, thank you.'

He eased himself away and shut her door, a spring in his step and a whistle on his lips as he jogged around to the driver's side of the car, thinking that this day was going to be full of surprises.

Laura lined up the ball. A miniature Uluru lay red and ominous at the end of the fuzzy green trail. This was the big one. The clincher. If she got this in one shot, the hat-trick would be hers.

'Looks like there's a bump about halfway along,' Ryan whispered in her ear.

She and Ryan had been conveniently teamed as a

pair—thanks, no doubt, to Jill, who owned the Tandarah Mini-golf links and thus was the organiser of the event.

Laura stood up straight and glared at him, amazed she was so close to winning considering he had been playing mental games with her all day. 'You seriously think I need coaching advice from *you*? And where is it likely you will come today?'

'Umm…about eighteenth, at last count.'

'Last. Eighteenth is last, Ryan. So keep your advice to yourself.'

He held up two hands in self-defence. 'Hey, I was just trying to ensure that the gold shirt is yours. I have a vested interest in this, remember?'

'Oh?'

'You promised I might be able to try one on, one day. I figure the more shirts you have, the more likely that honour will come about.'

'Come on, Mum!' Chloe called out from the sidelines. Her face was painted to look like a tiger, and she stood arm in arm with Tammy.

Laura sent her daughter a big smile, all the while remembering the way her little girl had taken hold of Ryan's hand back at the car. Ryan's face had come over all hazy and devoted, and she had known all her grand plans had come to nought. While she'd been running around, trying to sort out everyone else's muddles, Ryan and Chloe had become smitten with one another. The danger she had sensed was always just around the corner had arrived with a bang.

She took a deep calming breath, which did nothing at all to calm her, then leant over and lined up her bright orange ball once more. Now she only had to get over the fact that Ryan was standing behind her, his eyes no doubt focused on her wriggling…club.

She cleared her mind, looked at the fake red rock, looked at the ball, imagined it was Ryan's smirking face, and hit.

The ball skittered and jumped along the bumpy path, hit the wall about halfway and slowly meandered along the painted concrete towards the tiny hole at the base of Uluru. The small crowd standing along the edge of the 'fairway' took in a collective deep breath, all eyes following the ball as it skipped, rolled, and plopped with a perfect clunk into the waiting hole.

The crowd cheered. Laura leapt into the air, and was soon enveloped in a pair of strong arms. She squealed, all breath slamming from her body as she was twirled through the air. All thoughts of winning faded away as she revelled in the sensation of warm arms—male arms, Ryan's arms—wrapped tight about her. When he finally put her down he didn't let her go. His arm remained proprietorially about her waist as everyone congratulated her.

'My partner. She couldn't have done it without me,' he said, eliciting laughs all around from the other players, and giving a perfectly reasonable excuse for the two of them to remain snuggled together.

She didn't believe it for a second. There was more behind Ryan's casually positioned arm than sporting partnership. But what could she do? Throw his arm away and look unkind? Wrap both arms about his heavenly waist and look out of control? Or continue as she was, smiling and laughing and pretending that the skin along her waist wasn't burning up under his easy touch.

After several minutes of seductive torture Laura had cause to uncurl herself from Ryan's embrace as she went up onto the makeshift dais to accept her new shirt. As usual, it was gold, shiny, and excessively big. But, as usual, it gave her a particular thrill to have won. To have thrown herself into the game and won. She didn't do something purely for herself often enough.

She looked out into the crowd to see Chloe jumping up and down, yelling loudly, one hand tucked happily into Ryan's arm. And, seeing that tableau before her, Laura knew then that she had been kidding herself. Winning the mini-golf tournament was fun, but if she were ever able to choose something for herself she would choose this. She would choose someone to share her life. Someone with whom to share Chloe's growth. Someone with whom to match wits, share smiles, and give warmth. Someone real, strong, and fascinating. Someone very much like Ryan Gasper.

The odds against her were stacked too high. Firstly, he had never stayed put in one place longer than a month in his whole adult life. And, secondly, he was still Chloe's uncle. The way he had chastised himself after their kiss proved he would never really be able to see her as just Laura—woman in love.

Not wanting Chloe, or Ryan, to see how much that picture clenched at her heart, she grinned convincingly down at them. They both grinned back, and her heart ached all the more.

After all of the awards had been given—pretty much ensuring that every participant went home with some sort of trophy—Laura skipped down the stairs and made a beeline for her daughter. When she was within a few feet she grabbed Chloe by the hand and did not stop walking, hoping they would simply lose Ryan within the crowd. She needed time away from his overwhelming company. Time to convince herself she wasn't in love with him. She shouldn't be. She couldn't be.

'Do you want that candyfloss now, possum?'

'Yes, please!'

Laura looked back, and the smile dropped from her face when she saw that Chloe was leading Ryan on a baby elephant walk through the crowd.

'Don't you have any other families to bug right now?' Laura asked, as they approached Jill at the candyfloss stand.

'Perhaps,' he said, his sexy smooth voice sending glorious but entirely unwanted shivers through her torso, 'but the sound of candyfloss was too good to pass up.'

'Too much sugar and you'll lose all your teeth before you're forty.'

'Rubbish,' he said, his perfectly healthy teeth gleaming at her.

'Two sticks, please, Auntie Jill,' Chloe said.

'I don't know that you can stomach two sticks of floss, Chloe,' Jill said.

'No! One is for me and one is for Uncle Ryan.'

'Okay, then. So, champ,' Jill said, looking at Laura, 'are we having fun?' Her gaze flickered to a point over Laura's shoulder, and Laura wanted to reach out and strangle her meddling friend.

'Bucketloads,' she said, through gritted teeth.

'I think beating me guaranteed that,' Ryan said, tucking in beside her, resting a hand on Chloe's shoulder.

Jill's eagle eyes took in the scene. 'I'll bet,' she said. She handed over the first stick of sugary pink floss to Chloe. 'Now, don't eat it too fast.'

'Thanks, Auntie Jill. I won't…'

Something in Chloe's voice caught Laura's attention. Sweat slicked Chloe's forehead, melting the face paint, and she was breathing with her mouth open.

'You okay, babe?'

Chloe nodded, eyeing the floss with wide eyes, but Laura was not to be deterred.

'Do you have your puffer?' Laura asked.

Chloe nodded again, but this time pulled the blue and white contraption from the pocket at the front of her overalls and took a deep breath of medicine.

'Better?'

'Better.' Chloe took a lick of candyfloss, ending up with half of it on her nose. 'I'm going to meet Tammy on the merry-go-round. Is that okay?'

'Sure. Have fun.'

'She can have my candyfloss,' Ryan offered. 'An old man like me has to look after his teeth.'

'Thanks!' Chloe said, before running away with both pink fluffy sticks in her hand to find her friend.

Ryan wondered if a six-year-old city kid would think herself too old for such a ride, whereas sweet Chloe Somervale still had much childhood left in front of her. It was comforting that there was a place in the world where kids still found pleasure in skipping-ropes, pet dogs, and fairground rides.

Ryan watched Laura as she watched her daughter run through the maze of adult legs towards her friend on the other side of the park. There was something about her that kept him hooked. Something soft beneath her sharp wit. Something warm behind her cool gaze. Something deep beneath the blustery façade.

'I'm going to head off and do the washing-up from the barbecue, Jill,' Laura said, once Chloe was out of her sight.

'Don't be silly. I have staff to look after that.'

'Let them play today. I'm happy to do it.'

'There are always Doc Larson's boys. They are terrified of me. If I say the word, they'll do it. I'll keep an eye on Chloe; you two go off and enjoy the sunshine together.'

Ryan could see Laura was on edge. Her toes curled and uncurled in her sandals, her hands continuously tugged at the tie of her gold winner's shirt.

'Yeah,' he said. 'I reckon you could do with some sunshine right about now.'

She turned on him, her eyes flashing. 'I get *sunshine* enough at home, thank you very much.' And then she seemed to realise what she had intimated. 'Oh, blow the both of you,' she blurted, and took off, presumably to work out her frustrations in the kitchen.

Ryan watched her storm away. 'I can't keep up with her. I don't think even the Energizer bunny could keep up with her.'

'Well, handsome,' Jill said, 'I tell you what; I'm having no trouble keeping up with the game at hand.'

'Game?' he repeated.

'It's not as though he moved out and you moved right in,' she said. 'Time has passed. Wounds have healed. Look at the situation with an open mind. You are a man, she is a woman, and there is a little girl in between whom you both love very much.'

Ryan turned and stared at Jill, ready to tell her to mind her own damn business. But she wasn't grinning inanely at him, like some busybody. She was dead serious.

'I don't consider the sort of thing you are talking about a game, Jill.'

'Neither does she. So don't let her run away,' Jill said. 'You'll regret it.'

But Ryan was already on his way, so he didn't have a chance to rebuff or agree. 'Wait up, Laura!' he called as he caught up to her.

'I'm busy.'

'And I'm handy with a teatowel.'

'Good for you.'

They reached the kitchen where the Upper Gum Tree Hotel met the mini-golf links. Ryan jumped forward and held open the door, then followed her into the blissfully cool and quiet room.

She twirled her long hair into a makeshift ponytail, grabbed a pair of elbow-length washing gloves, without even having to look where they were, and swished her hands under the tap water to find the perfect temperature. Then she threw a teatowel at him and he caught it.

'I like your friends,' he said. 'It's a pretty great community here.'

'They have their moments.'

'Meaning?' he asked.

'Well, Chloe came home upset from school the other day, because apparently you are not her uncle, you are an American movie star out here *under cover*. You are divorced and hiding from the law because you stole that ridiculous car of yours. And that's all just from Chloe's schoolmates.'

'Wow. I had no idea they'd found me out so soon!'

Her mouth twitched into a fleeting smile, but by the vigour of her scouring he knew it mattered to her that the three of them had become fodder for the town gossips.

There must have been plenty of talk when she'd first found out she was pregnant, and she'd had to bear it alone. Anger bubbled to the surface as he wished he could have been there to shield her from any talk. From any hurt. But instead his presence here now was only bringing it all swarming back. 'I'm truly sorry,' he said.

She gazed back at him, her big pale brown eyes clear and bright. 'For what?'

'For putting you in a situation where you have to deal with gossip. Again. From what I've deduced, you have an amazing standing in this town. I only hope that my being here hasn't maligned the reputation you have worked so hard to uphold.'

'Don't be silly. Let them talk. My life is my own. What I get up to is my business. The people who I care about, who care about me, love me no matter what. The rest is just white noise.'

She was nobody's fool, and the most beguiling, surprising, courageous woman he had ever known. And the most fidgety. He wondered what it would take to make her stop, to halt time, to give her a moment to catch her breath. He had recently learned how liberating it felt to let his head roll back and drink the rain. He wondered how long it had been since she had allowed herself such an indulgence. Then there was the way she had reacted, the way she had melted and given in to her most basic desires when they had kissed… The time had come to find out many things.

'Have dinner with me, Laura,' he asked. 'A real date.'

Without even looking at him she answered, 'No. Nope. Can't. Won't.' But he could see that her hands had stopped washing and had gripped the sink.

Ryan reached out and tucked the tumble of curls over her shoulder. He didn't want her hiding behind her hair. 'You really can, Laura. I'm certain Jill, or Tammy's mum, will happily babysit Chloe. I can drive us into town. We order. We eat. We don't talk about Will. We don't talk about Chloe. We only talk about us, and this exceptional attraction between us. Easy as pie.'

Laura shook her head. 'Pie isn't easy, Ryan. I for one should know. Sometimes it has apples, as well as blueberries, and it can be quite a big deal to get it just right. And that's not even considering the pastry.'

She was babbling. That was the last way to sway him from wanting to spend time with her. 'Well, let's defy convention,' he said. 'Let's make it easy. Man and woman go on date. One date. One evening together to see if we should even think about taking this thing between us further…'

Laura spun on her heels and pierced him with a wild glare. 'You just don't get it, do you? The answer is no. I can't go on a date with you.' She stumbled to a stop as she gathered her thoughts, and Ryan steeled himself. 'The fact is, it tears me up inside every time I see you fixing another fence or wrangling your goats. Because I know, in my heart of hearts, that though it's all fun and games right now, you *will* return to your real life. Right now you're benefiting from being here—reconnecting with Will, playing house, playing Mr Fix-it, playing dad, and playing with the farm-girl's helpless heart. But it won't last.'

'Laura, don't—'

'No, you started this, but now I have to finish it. The other morning, before I found you asleep with Munchkin, I thought you had gone. That you had left. And it… I couldn't breathe. My chest hurt so bad I didn't know what to think. The idea that someone else I…that another person in my life could leave so suddenly was too hard to take. I can't do it again. The risk is just too great. Because this time it isn't just about my risk, or my heart. I never want Chloe to have to experience the pain of abandonment. I will not let you do that to her.'

Whoa. Ryan had had no idea how deep her anguish ran. He loved Kardinyarr and her challenges more every day. But he wasn't going to lie to himself, or her. She had fair reason to worry. He still woke up every morning thinking through the daily itinerary of the convention he should have been attending in Las Vegas. He wondered what his mates were doing on the other side of the world as he rounded up his livestock. He was happy where he was, but would he never want to leave? He really couldn't say. But at least he was willing to have an open mind about it. He had learned that from his stubborn little brother: never say never.

'Laura, I won't let you push me away like this. I am not Will.' Even as he said it, Ryan knew it was the wrong thing to say. Her lovely face closed over and all thoughts were locked behind an icy glare.

'I know you're not. You are nothing like him. Will was undemanding, and kind, and he knew he wasn't perfect. Whereas you—you are invulnerable, and intoxicating, and you are too bloody perfect!'

He crushed his hands between his back and the sink, knowing that if he gave in to the urge to reach out to her she would as likely bite his fingers as not. 'Laura, nobody's perfect. I have done and said things in my life I wish I could take back.'

'Well, I haven't. I don't regret a thing I have done. Not a word I have said. I'm a good person. I go out of my way to make sure that I hurt nobody in my life. When I sent Will I was doing the right thing, the proper thing, in letting him go. I know it.' Her shoulders slumped, and his vibrant tempestuous Laura looked so small and so frail.

Putting aside all thoughts of his own safety, Ryan closed the gap between them and rested his hands on her shoulders, his fingers caressing the fine hollows beneath her neck. 'Sweetheart, don't do this to yourself.

You can't help it if you are so utterly lovely that men fall over themselves to be with you. We have no control over our own hearts, much less over anybody else's.'

He turned her around and she didn't fight him. Using one finger, he lifted her chin so she had no choice but to look him in the eye. 'Laura, it's time to stop running. Only if you stop running can any of us hope to catch up with you.'

He could feel the warmth of her body radiating towards him, calling him, beckoning him. Then she looked at him. Really looked at him. Her eyes skittered, blinked, and then shone. And with a telling sigh she stood on tiptoes, slid her sudsy gloved hands around his neck, and kissed him.

Her kiss was so sudden it caught him off guard. His heart slammed against his ribs. Or perhaps it was her heart. Her ribs. Then just as suddenly his body came to life, every inch of him pulsing as her soft lips pressed against his, coaxing, imploring, summoning him to give in as she had.

He did as he was asked and let the commotion overwhelm him. He let her lead. Let her guide him beyond attraction to something deeper, more honest, and infinitely more fulfilling than he had expected from a woman who only moments before had been determined to deny him.

With a heavy groan he wrapped his arms about her small frame, lifting her until her toes barely touched the ground. She turned limp in his arms, the kiss softening and intensifying at the same time.

Ryan could barely breathe. He saw nothing behind his eyes, but he felt with each nerve in his body every whisper of her breath, every tremor down her length.

Giddy with pleasure, and slightly losing balance, he

bumped Laura against the bench behind her and their lips slid apart. There they stood, looking into one another's eyes, their ragged breaths mixing as their lips rested mere millimetres apart. Dribbles of soapy water ran down his back, his raw nerves shivering in response. Ryan finally let her feet slide to the floor.

'I promised myself I wouldn't do that,' she said, and when she blinked two perfect shimmering tracks of silver slid down her cheeks.

'Oh, God, Laura…'

She lifted a finger and held it to his lips. 'Don't.'

Don't what? he wondered. Don't apologise? Don't tell her the depth of what he was feeling? Don't kiss her again?

The sound of voices outside permeated their warm bubble and Laura pushed him away, quickly straightening her clothes and wiping away her tears. But she could not wipe away all evidence of their kiss. Her lips were swollen and moist, her cheeks were too pink, and her eyes were round and shell-shocked.

Father Grant came blustering into the room with Chloe on his back. 'Laura, I found this creature making dirt castles outside with a couple of the local boys.'

When he saw the two of them, Father Grant stopped short. 'Oh, Mr Gasper. Good evening.'

'Evening, Father.'

'So, when do we get to meet the rest of your family?' Father Grant asked, filling the loaded silence as best he could. 'I am a huge fan of your sister's.'

'Jen would love to know that,' Ryan said.

Father Grant summoned up a decent blush. 'Ah, actually I meant Samantha. I am a closet quilter from long back. I do hope that now you've found us, you will be bringing the rest of your intriguing family for a visit.'

'There are more of them?' Chloe asked.

Laura held out her arm and, taking Chloe by a dirty hand, held her tight in front of her. 'There's more of them,' Laura said. Her voice was still shaky. 'Ryan has two sisters as well.'

'Wow!' Chloe said. 'I bet I have a bigger family than even Tammy now!'

Ryan knew Laura was using the little girl as a shield. She had told him in no uncertain terms that she hadn't wanted to kiss him again. No, not that she hadn't wanted to kiss him, but that she *wouldn't* kiss him. So she had thought about it. But instead of choosing to enjoy the raging, straining, impossible-to-ignore attraction that had grabbed hold of the both of them, she was desperate to renounce it. And for good reason.

What was he really thinking of, hitting on a single mother? Falling harder and harder for the mother of his brother's child? Maybe since he was the one with the least to lose it should be up to him to put an end to it. If it was causing her that much distress, enough to bring tears to those big shining eyes, he had to stop. Stop the torrent of feelings that overwhelmed him every time he caught sight of her? No. But stop letting her know about it. That he could hopefully do.

She had cared enough for Will to let him go. Knowing it was her deepest wish, he had no choice but to give her the same gift.

Chloe gripped her mother's arms, yawning with a wide open mouth.

'Time to go home?' he asked, his voice soft, letting them both off the hook.

Laura nodded. 'Can you let Jill know she might need Doc Larson's boys to finish up here, after all?' Laura asked Father Grant. 'It's time I took this one home.'

'Sure. Of course. You guys head home.'

'You ready?' Laura asked, looking down into her daughter's tired face with such easy love Ryan felt his heart squeeze in his chest.

He would drive them home, and for the next little while he would leave it at that. A couple of days without contact would surely staunch the fires.

Surely…

CHAPTER NINE

LAURA sat tucked up on the window-seat in her bedroom, the curtain hooked behind her back so she could stare out of the window at the star-spangled night. How could she possibly have fallen in love with Will's brother? She twirled a piece of orange twine around her fingers as her mind buzzed and whirred, looking for an answer, a way out. How could she possibly have fallen in love with Will's brother?

The shoebox lay open on the seat at her feet. Newspaper clippings spilled over the cushion, as well as a dried wild flower Will had picked for her on one of their long walks around Kardinyarr. It felt like so long ago. And she could not even remember the significance of the twine, which she had found at the bottom of the box. Had that been in the box to start with? Or had she and Will created a long-forgotten memory around it?

She disentangled the twine and pressed it back into the box, along with the other bits and pieces that one day Chloe would hold dear—these simple treasures mapping the significant friendship between a couple of kids.

But her love for Ryan was the love of a woman. She was in love with his strengths, and with his frailties. She was in love with the intensity of his wish to be a good man. She was in love with the way he adored her daughter. She was in love with the way he kissed. She was in love with his dark curls, with his beautiful blue eyes, with the way he filled out his fading blue jeans.

She'd meant to pull back, denying her feelings, knowing they did not serve either of them well. Kissing him again probably hadn't been the best way to achieve those ends. But, oh, what a kiss. Laura rubbed her lips together, closed her eyes, and relived those heavenly moments. She'd known the whole time she was wrapped in his strong embrace that it was the kiss of a lifetime. Heavenly. Perfect. And heartbreaking. It would never happen again. It had been enough to make her weep.

Uncurling her limbs, she slipped off the seat, let the curtain fall back into place and moved to her bed. Sleep was a fool's errand, but she should at least rest.

But just as she drew the sheet up to her chin she heard it.

A wheeze.

She was out of bed and at Chloe's side before the little one had taken her third strained breath.

'Chloe—wake up.' She gave her daughter a light shake, waking her from her troubled slumber.

Chloe's eyes shot open and her eyes all but bulged from her face. Laura brought her into a sitting position, grabbed the reliever puffer from beside the bed, and held it to Chloe's mouth. 'Here, possum, take a deep breath.'

She repeated this four times, but the wheezing did not abate. The ventilator controlling the temperature, the moisture levels and pollens in the room was humming away happily, but it wasn't enough. She had Chloe take a second series of puffs, but it made no difference. Laura knew her daughter could not long survive such a lack of oxygen-fuelled breaths.

She ran to the phone and called Dr Gabriel, who lived twenty kilometres away. 'Come on, come on,' she begged into the phone as it rang and rang. With her spare hand, she tore off her nightie and slipped into a T-shirt and soft track pants, ready to go at a moment's notice. Dr Gabriel's mobile answered.

'Gabe, it's Laura. Chloe is having a pretty bad attack.'

'Laura?' She heard the stress in his voice from that one word and her heart-rate doubled. 'Cindy Mathews is having her baby at home. There have been complications. I can't leave.' There was a pause, then, 'Look, get in the car. Bring Chloe here.'

The Mathews farm was thirty kilometres past Doc's place. An hour's drive at least. Not good enough.

'Thanks, Gabe. But I don't know that there's time. I'll find another way to get help. You just concentrate on Cindy, and tell her from me that it's all worth it.'

'Shall do.' The good doctor hung up and Laura was left alone in her small stifling house, with her little daughter gasping for breath.

She ran a hand over Chloe's forehead, smoothing out her damp hair, trying to calm her as much as possible. 'It's okay, sweetie. Mummy's going to get you help.'

Laura squeezed her brain for a way out. A plan. She called on all her motherly instincts to find an answer.

'Mum…' Chloe called, her voice wheezing, on the verge of panic.

It was enough to kick Laura's instincts into overdrive. She grabbed her little girl into her arms, kicked open the front door and ran across the moonlit patch of dirt and dying grass to her last hope.

Ryan shifted in his sleep. A loud continued knocking came at his door and his eyes flew open. It occurred to him that the knocking had been going on for some time, and it was what had woken him in the first place.

Throwing off his hot sheet, he dragged his half-asleep body to the back door to find Laura standing in his doorway, in a pink T-shirt and track pants, her hair wild and curling about her face. His first thought was *gorgeous*… How could he possibly hope to deny his attraction to her?

But then he saw the terror in her eyes. Chloe lay sideways across her arms, her head tucked into her mother's shoulder. And the little girl was wheezing, pulling for breaths that just wouldn't come.

'She can't breathe,' Laura said, on the verge of panic. 'I can't lose her. Don't let me lose her, too.'

Ryan stepped forward to… He knew not what. To take the girl from her mother's arms? Never. To give the girl the breath from his own lungs? He figured that would not help, or Laura would have done as much already.

'What can I do?' he asked, feeling more helpless than ever in his life before.

'Your plane,' she said, her words spare and fast. 'You have to fly us to the Woondarah Hospital.'

Right. He could do that. 'Come in, come in,' he said, taking her by the shoulder and drawing her into his home.

Laura shook her head. 'We'll be at your car.'

With a curt nod, Ryan ran into his bedroom, whipped on a pair of jeans, shoved his feet into sandshoes and grabbed a shirt, slinging it over his shoulders without bothering to button it up. He grabbed the keys to Betsy, shut his front door without locking it, and then ran to his car.

Laura was already there, running soothing hands over Chloe's hair and making constant cooing noises. When she heard Ryan's footsteps, she looked up at him, and her eyes were frantic. Her long auburn curls whipped about her face. He had never seen anything more beautiful or more heart-wrenching. Staunching the hit of inescapable affection, he pulled open the rear door to the car, slammed it shut once Laura and Chloe were in place, leapt into the front seat, and tore off down the dirt driveway.

'How close is Woondarah Hospital to an airstrip?' he asked.

'Not at all. But there is a golf course right alongside it. Couldn't we land there?'

A golf course. Little chance of powerlines. His Betsy could handle a bush landing, no worries, so long as she had the landing distance and a well-lit runway…

Ignoring road rules, he was on his mobile to the Mackay place within the minute. He kept his voice low and calm as he explained the situation at hand, and was relieved almost to the point of tears when Frank Mackay agreed to get on to the local control tower, declaring Ryan's intention to pilot a low-altitude mercy flight from the Mackay airfield to Woondarah Hospital. Frank promised to have the permission and the flight plan ready when they arrived. Anything for that sweet Laura Somervale.

He shot furtive glances at Laura as his sports car ate up the short mile to the airstrip in record time. Her face was drawn. Her eyes were wide and unblinking. Her cheeks were pale and tight. She was petrified.

The car skidded to a halt by the side of the small plane, and Laura was out of the car before he was. Frank was waiting for them, and he talked Ryan through every step of the journey as they loaded up the plane. Frank assured Ryan that he had checked, and his airframe and fuel levels were appropriate—which saved him some time.

Ryan reached out, and Laura readily gave up her precious cargo into his waiting arms. He cradled Chloe's head as he slipped her into a seat and buckled her in. The poor little thing was shivering, cold, terrified. Ryan gulped down a lump in his throat as he pushed her damp curls from her sweating forehead. 'We're taking you to help, possum. It won't be long now.'

Chloe smiled at Ryan's use of her pet name, and he took that as a happy sign. With no time for gallant assistance, he leapt from the plane, grabbed Laura around the waist and hoisted her up into the back seat, ignoring the pleasure of her smooth curves against his palms. He slammed the door shut, wrenched open the door to the cabin and hopped in. He shot Frank a thankful salute, then the plane was rumbling to life.

He finished his post-start and pre-flight checks as he taxied to the downwind end of the runway. Precious minutes later, after performing essential idle-speed checks and run-ups, they were in the air. Once cruising he shot a glance over his shoulder. 'You okay back there?'

Laura nodded, though her eyes looked wide and fearful. He only wished he could go faster, harder, quicker, get her down sooner. But instead he slowed his reactions and followed procedure of Night Visual Flight Rules. It would get them there safe and sound, and that was more important.

He relayed information to Laura all the way there. Keeping her up to date on their estimated time of arrival, with his conversations with the hospital, with their altitude, everything. He only hoped it helped, that it felt as if they were getting closer.

Within fifteen minutes they were in sight of the hospital. He only hoped Frank's plan had worked. His eyes skittered over the ground ahead and he saw it..the pale glow of the hospital roof, with its helipad lit nice and bright. To the west of the hospital was the golf course, and there it was—the glow from thirty sets of car headlights, switched to full beam, pointing slightly into the wind so as not to blind him as they lit the ninth fairway for him.

As the fates had it, the Woondarah Golf Links had held a wedding reception that night and, upon hearing news of the mercy flight, every member of the party with a car had turned out onto the fairway to help.

Betsy landed like a dream, with the least amount of bumps he could have hoped for considering their makeshift runway. As the plane rumbled to a halt, its tyres kicking up great hunks of the perfect grass, Ryan saw an ambulance heading towards him. Inside would be a trauma crew, ready and waiting. He ripped off his headphones, leapt out of the plane and around, to help Chloe down.

He blanched. The little girl was colourless. She had stopped breathing. He held her limp form for only moments before the hospital crew took her from him and rushed her across the oval in the mini-ambulance to the hospital next door.

He dragged his eyes back up towards the plane, to find Laura slumped against the seat, tears pouring down her face. She was spent. He had never seen anything like it. Never experienced anything so…real.

He had avoided Will's funeral, sensing he would not cope. Knowing the sight of a coffin with his brother inside it would break him into a thousand pieces that would never be put back again. But this woman had been there. Within two months of losing her father she had pulled herself together enough to be there for Will.

He hadn't known what responsibility meant before

he'd met her. It didn't just mean creating reports, giving speeches to ensure his findings were heard. It didn't mean accepting every talking engagement that ever came his way in an effort to change the world for the better. It didn't even mean telling someone when you knew they were wrong. Responsibility meant being there for another person. It meant looking out for their most urgent as well as their lesser needs. It meant looking out for their happiness and their well-being. It meant thinking of someone other than yourself.

Laura had lost too many loved ones already in her short lifetime, and now her daughter was in a critical condition. How she managed to remain lucid he had no idea. His heart was beating so fast he felt faint. And angry. And exhausted. And helpless. He itched to get onto his mobile and call his folks, and his sisters, just to hear their voices. Later. He would certainly do so later.

But in that moment he had no other choice but to reach up and take Laura in his arms, comfort her, ease her pain, carry her inside the hospital towards her healing daughter.

Ryan sat in the hospital waiting room, waiting, and watching the line of early-morning sunlight creep under the frosted-glass doors.

He tried to think if he had missed anything. Laura had given him a list of phone numbers, so everybody was up to date. Jill knew where they all were. Dr Gabriel had been assured they had made it okay. Doc Larson, the local vet, would call in on the goats, and would organise one of their closer neighbours to check up on them and feed them later in the day as well. Nice people.

All of them. He was practically a stranger to them, but still they'd banded together without pause to help.

His tired eyes misted over, and he'd almost managed to zone out the sounds of shuffling feet, sniffling patients, clanking utensils and the smell of antiseptic and floor cleaner, when he felt a small tap on his shoulder. He looked up to find a kindly nurse smiling down upon him.

'Mr Gasper?'

He nodded.

'Ms Somervale hoped you might join her in Chloe's room.'

He stood, running his palms down the front of his jeans. 'Where do I go?'

The nurse pointed the way. Ryan took several deep breaths and went to find his girls.

Laura sat on a vinyl chair, her chin resting against her hands, which clasped Chloe's hands. Chloe looked so small in the big white bed. But though she looked pale, she was breathing of her own accord as she slept.

'Is she okay?' he asked.

Laura lifted her head and nodded. 'She stopped breathing for about a minute.' She shuddered. 'But the doctors performed their magic, and she's now breathing steadily. She fell asleep a few minutes ago.' Laura's eyes drifted shut. 'Maybe I should move into the city. But then again Melbourne has one of the highest concentrations of allergens in the world, so not Melbourne. But closer to a hospital at least. What do you think?'

She looked up at him with her big, beseeching eyes, and, though he gave his considered opinion to heads of state and to Fortune 500 companies every day, he had never felt as honoured to be asked in all his life. He crouched down next to her chair and laid a hand over hers, feeling her life force as well as Chloe's flow through him.

'Laura, stay. She loves Tandarah. That's her home. And she came out of this just fine.'

'We can hardly rely on you being nearby with a handy plane any time this happens again.'

'Why not?'

She swallowed. 'Come on, Ryan…'

It all came back to her concerns in the kitchen at the Upper Gum Tree. Despite everything else, despite their pasts, despite their familial relationship, it all came to nought if he wasn't sticking around.

Laura's gaze locked onto his and held. He knew that she was thinking back and forth to the pros and cons of that occurrence. Having him stay meant that Chloe would have family all around her. Having him stay meant Chloe would be that much more safe living in her beloved town. But having him stay would mean no more excuses. They could not hope distance would temper the feelings they had for one another.

'Anyway,' he said, 'now is not the time to settle any of this. I've found us a room. There's a motel a couple of blocks from here.' He knew she was going to refuse, so he made it easier for her to say yes. 'Somewhere to take a nap. A shower. Have some peace. You'll be no good to Chloe when she wakes if you can't even gather the energy to crack your sunshiny smile.'

He reached out, tucking his hand beneath her ear and running his thumb along the fine smile line on her cheek. It was enough to encourage the line to deepen as she managed a crooked smile. Ryan even imagined that she pressed against his palm. For a brief second he believed it, believed that she rubbed her cheek against his hand before gently pulling away.

'Thanks, Ryan. A shower would be wonderful.'

* * *

An hour later, Ryan came in from the local twenty-four-hour market with a bag full of staples. He had bought food, aloe vera tissues, and clean underwear for himself.

He had planned to get some for Laura too, but that had been beyond him, standing staring at a wall full of multi-coloured, different-sized women's underwear. As soon as somebody else had begun to trundle a trolley up his aisle he had choked and given up.

He went back to the motel with a plan to send her straight out shopping for them on her own, but when he arrived she was fast asleep on the bed. She wore a white cotton robe. Her heavy auburn curls were splayed out over the pillow. Her face shone from being scrubbed clean and glowed pink from the warmth in the room.

Ryan quietly laid the bags on the kitchenette table and went into the bathroom to clean up. He stopped short when he happened upon her underwear, which was drying on the shower rail. Fine, lacy, white—and evocative. He did his best to ignore it. And the fact that it meant that beneath the white cotton robe Laura was completely bare.

He looked at himself in the mirror. 'Okay, *Cowboy*. Hands off. She is exhausted. Her daughter is in hospital. She took up your offer of a bed and a shower only to be alert for her daughter, not for any other reason you might have in mind.'

Drawing in a deep, ragged breath, he walked out into the cosy room where Laura slept. Looking down upon her, he felt his promise to himself fast slipping away. The woman was a total beauty. With an attitude that said *hands off* but an innate sweetness that said *hold me.*

Ryan fought harder than ever before against the mixed messages.

He sat down on the edge of the bed. The springs creaked, but she didn't even stir. Yet when Chloe's breathing had hitched earlier in the night she had heard it all. It was as though she knew her daughter was safe now, so she could sleep.

The sun had fully risen, and it filtered through a gap in the heavy orange curtains, spilling a glowing sliver of light across the bed and onto the bright bronze highlights in Laura's hair.

Unable to help himself, Ryan reached out and wrapped a clump of curls about his hand. The cool skein slipped softly over his fingers. He could smell the scent of the sweet pineapple juice she had drunk at the hospital easing from between her lips with her soft, slow breaths.

'Laura…Laura,' he whispered. 'Surely it's no accident that we have ended up here together. What if the many decisions in our lives have led us to this point for a reason? What if you were meant to meet Will to give Chloe life? And what if I was meant to find your letter only at the precise moment I was able to take the time to find you, and you were ready to give your heart to someone new? Did you ever think of that?'

She stirred, her body stretching, her limbs sliding across the bed as she woke. A small moan slid from her mouth as her eyes flickered open. Then she raised one thin arm to shield her sleepy eyes from the burgeoning sunlight.

'Hi,' she said, her voice husky and sexy as hell.

Ryan swallowed to wet his parched throat. 'Good morning, sunshine.'

Laura's mouth stretched into a long yawn, and mid-way through she took in her surroundings: beige wallpaper, orange curtains, double bed, a table with two chairs. The décor screamed small-chain motel. And then she remembered why. Chloe. Before she even moved off the bed, Ryan held up his mobile phone.

'I just called the hospital,' he said. 'She's still asleep and they don't expect her to wake for another couple of hours. So I reckon we have until about nine o'clock before we need to head back.'

Laura sat up, carefully tucking the robe about her thighs and across her chest, wondering how long he had been sitting on the end of the bed watching her. She had felt it in her sleep, which was why she had woken so languorous and warm.

She shook her head. 'I've rested enough. I think I'd prefer to have a quick shower and head back now.'

'Wearing what?' Ryan asked.

Laura looked over to her track pants and T-shirt, hanging over the back of a chair, then her glance slid to the bathroom door, behind which her lacy white underwear dripped tap water slowly onto the bathroom floor.

'You make a fair point,' Laura conceded, sinking her face into her palms. 'I'm not thinking straight right now.'

'That's perfectly understandable.'

'So what can I do for two hours with no dry underwear?' The minute the words came out of her mouth she wished she could take them back.

She waited for Ryan to take advantage, to crack a joke, to smile that cheeky smile that made her insides squirm. He wanted her. She knew that for a fact. And after the way she had thrown herself at him he knew she wanted him too.

But instead, after several moments of sustained eye contact, during which time Laura imagined too many ways to spend such time, Ryan stood and walked over to the table.

He grabbed two grocery bags and began to pull out all sorts of goodies. 'For now,' he said, holding up a packet of fresh bread rolls, salad ingredients and fresh-cut cold meats, 'we eat. And once we are full, and your underwear is dry, we can go back to Chloe revitalised and refreshed and ready to cheer her up so she won't even remember she's in a hospital.' He pulled a pack of playing cards and a funny-looking little fluffy bear from the grocery bags as well. 'It's all they had,' he apologised.

Laura shuffled over to the table, tucking one foot beneath her and taking hold of the fluffy bear. She buried her face into its soft fur. 'It's beautiful.'

She watched Ryan as he chopped and sliced, creating the most imaginative mountain of a sandwich she had ever seen. He had mentioned a cooking speciality once, and it seemed she was now being allowed to witness it. He slid the finished product her way, using a paper grocery bag as a plate. Then he sat in the chair next to hers and watched her take her first bite.

'Good, huh?'

'This is fantastic,' she said, with a mouthful of bread.

'That's pretty high praise coming from the best cook I have ever known.'

Ryan took a bite of his, and the two of them chewed in comfortable silence until they were all done. Laura moved to clean up, but Ryan pressed her back into her chair.

She watched him do the job that was usually hers, and thoroughly enjoyed the guilty pleasure of being waited upon. She felt spoilt. She felt cared for. She felt so much love for him she could barely contain herself.

'Where did you come up with this concoction?' she asked, her adoring eyes following him around the room.

'Living out of hotels, one has to come up with quick-fix healthy meals or one will turn sumo-wrestler-sized from eating too much Room Service food.'

When he seemed convinced the room was clean he turned back to face her. 'And now for the next instalment in the get-Laura-ready game. How does a too hot bubble bath sound?'

Like a dream come true! 'Are you serious?'

He delved into his bag of magic tricks and pulled out a mermaid-shaped bottle of bubble bath. 'It was either this, or some grotesque monster that I am sure is meant to encourage naughty, dirty eight-year-old boys to bathe. This seemed more you.'

'It's wonderful. It's perfect. Thank you, Ryan,' she managed to choke out.

'Come on, sunshine.' He took her by the elbow, led her into the bathroom, turned on the bath taps, poured in half the bottle of suds, walked back out into the bedroom, and closed the door, leaving her with the memory of the most doting smile she had ever received.

She leant her head against the back of the door. *Thank you, sweetheart. Gorgeous, darling man,* she wanted to add. But, at the post, her legendary courage failed her.

Ten minutes later, Ryan's mobile rang. He answered it.

'Gasper!' a familiar voice called at the other end.

'James Carlisle,' Ryan said to the personal financial advisor to a British publishing doyenne.

'I was sure I'd hear the magical ding-ding-ding of poker machines in the background.'

'I'm not in Las Vegas, James.'

'You bailed? On Vegas?'

'Something came up back in Australia. Now, what can I do for you, mate?'

'It's time, buddy. It's only taken me four years, but I have convinced the big kahuna to meet with you. Now is your big chance to pitch the book idea you've been beating my ears with all these years.'

Ryan looked over at the closed bathroom door. He heard a splash of water as Laura shifted her body beneath the bubbles.

'Ryan? I need you on a plane tonight. She has a half-hour window in two days' time. She wants a face-to-face pitch. Think talk-shows, spin-off book deals... Your feet will never touch solid ground again!'

And then, through the bathroom door, Ryan heard Laura begin to hum. The tune was recognisable, somewhat, as the Pirate King's theme song from *Pirates of Penzance*. The next weekend it would be the big show. If he hoofed it to London he would miss it. Worse, he would miss her.

'I'm sorry, James,' he said. 'I'm going to have to decline.'

The pause on the other end of the phone was heavy with shock. 'You're kidding, right?'

'No, mate. I have another couple of projects I'm working on back here. They've reached critical mass. I can't leave.'

'Projects bigger than this one? They must be something else. Anything I can get in on?'

The thought of suit-and-tie James out in the paddock with his goats made him grin. He thought of Munchkin taking her first steps. He thought of Jill Tucker and her cheeky banter. He thought of the new article resting on his laptop back home—the one he had started to write the day he had come home from the Minbah markets.

That article was fast turning into enough for a whole book in itself. A book he'd be excited to write. A book that needed many more months of hands-on research. Maybe years worth. Maybe a lifetime's worth.

He faced facts. For a guy who had lived in planes and high-rise hotels for the better part of his life, he found he actually loved the feel of solid ground beneath his feet. Will's words came swimming back to him.

This is her home, and as such it feels like my home too.

Kardinyarr was home because Laura Somervale was there.

'Not your kind of thing, James,' he said. 'But I'll let you know how I get on.'

'Do that, Ryan. Hope it all works out for you. Even though I now have to go and tell the big kahuna that the guy I've been raving about all these years has taken a better offer.'

At that moment Laura came out of the bathroom, all dressed, clean and hairdryer dried underwear hidden beneath her soft clothes, her hair up in the ubiquitous towel. Her face was pink and damp, and tiny curls crept from beneath the towel around her head. She continued to hum as she rubbed the moisture from her hair.

'It's the best offer this guy's ever had,' Ryan said.

'Good luck to you, then. I'll see you, Ryan,' James said.

'Count on it,' Ryan said, before hanging up the phone.

Laura turned at the sound of his voice. 'Was that the hospital?' she asked.

He shook his head. 'A friend overseas.'

'Anything important?'

'In the grand scheme of things?' He shook his head again. 'So, how was your bath? Too hot?'

She grinned, her whole face softening at the remembrance. 'Oh, yeah. I wouldn't care if my fingers and toes remained pruney for evermore. It was that good. And now that I have been thoroughly and undeservedly spoilt, let's go see my darling daughter and your darling niece.' She looked at him, her eyes imploring, as though half afraid he had another pamper session up his sleeve.

'Let's go get our girl.'

Laura clapped her hands together and, despite apparently promising herself that she would never kiss him again, planted a long hard kiss upon his mouth—a kiss filled with thanks, and desire, and so much more—before running back into the bathroom to dry her hair. And Ryan knew there was a lot he would do to get that reaction from this woman again. And again. And again.

CHAPTER TEN

ONE night, a week later, Ryan walked into a war zone.

Dishes lined Laura's sink. Chloe's clothes were strewn across the back of every sofa. The range hood still ran, though it was obvious dinner was long since finished. And the record player creaked and groaned as it came to the end of a record.

Laura ran from out of a doorway, dressed in her pirate costume, those tight purple pants doing it for him yet again.

'Evening, Laura.'

She looked up and seemed to light up when she saw him. But then she blinked furiously, doing her best to staunch the fire. But he knew better than to worry. 'Oh, Ryan. I wasn't sure that you would… I haven't seen you much these last few days.'

'I've been busy,' he said.

She spun on the spot, lifting sofa cushions as though looking for something. 'Bah! Doing what?'

'All sorts of things I think you would approve of. Farm things. Including trading in my *ridiculous* car for a new Ute.'

That stopped her fussing. She glanced up at him, her heavily mascara-rimmed eyes staring at him. Unblinking, shocked, and, just as he had hoped, thrilled to bits.

'You…really? Your car is gone?'

'Not gone from the neighbourhood, I fear. I've heard on the grapevine that Doc Larson's boys were going to pitch in to buy the car together. So if you see it coming down the road towards you, look out.'

'Well, the grapevine is usually right.'

'Hmm.'

As she looked at him, she took in a deep breath, her whole chest filling and releasing. Her beautiful golden-brown eyes glimmered back at him, and he knew she felt as breathless as he did. She blinked, looked away, and went back to her search with a vengeance. But he still knew better than to worry.

'Nevertheless, Mr Busy Man,' she said, 'you shouldn't just up and disappear like that. People worry.'

'People?' he asked.

'Chloe. Chloe has missed you.'

Her shoulders relaxed as she found a big, silver hoop earring. She stuck the pin into her ear as she bustled past him, doing all she could to ignore the inevitable electricity arcing between them. 'I am sorry. Can't talk now. Chloe is refusing to get dressed. And if I'm not there in the next fifteen minutes I am going to have a dozen ladies in pirate costumes going bananas.'

'You go. I still have to change and get ready yet. How about I take Chloe in a little while?'

Ryan thought she might hesitate, and he would have understood it if she had. If she agreed to leave Chloe in his care that would be the ultimate trust. But she merely smiled her great, glorious, sunshiny smile and he felt her trust light him from within.

'That would be much appreciated. The show starts at eight sharp.'

He nodded. 'That really means about twenty past, right?' he said.

Her gorgeous dimple showed itself before disappearing just as quickly. 'So it seems that you are starting to live on country time. Maybe we'll make a farmer of you after all.'

Sweetheart, you already have, he thought. 'Are you ready?'

She lifted a hand to her hair, felt the bandana still in place, and nodded. 'I've been ready for so long I can't remember if I'm really actually ready.'

'Go. Go on. We'll see you there in a little while.'

Laura grabbed her keys and her handbag and ran out through the door. She snuck her head back in to say, 'I'm glad you're back, Ryan.' Then she ran off before he could tell her he felt the same way.

Ryan headed down the hallway to find Chloe lying back on her bed reading. He leant in the doorway. 'Ms Somervale?'

Chloe snapped to attention, her startled gaze flickering to the open doorway behind her. 'Ryan. Where… where's Mum?'

'Gone to the theatre.'

Her bottom lip jutted out as she took in this pearl of information. It seemed that her spat had not worked as she had hoped.

'So, how about you get dressed so we can go and watch her sing up a storm to raise money for the drought-stricken farmers.'

Chloe was about to open her mouth to say no, but then, somehow, the whole big picture came clear. 'That's why she's singing tonight?'

'Yep.'

'Kylie at school. Her family lost all their calves last spring,' she said. 'She had to borrow her older sister's shoes for school all year, and they were too big for her. Some of the other kids laughed at her, but I just thought it was sad. I made Mum give her some shoes of mine I knew would fit her better.'

Ryan tried very hard to keep the indulgent grin from his face. *Like mother like daughter,* he thought. No matter how hard Chloe was trying to throw a tantrum, she had too much goodness bred into her for it to really work.

'Well, then, you had better come along and cheer louder than anybody so that your mum can help other kids like Kylie. Okay?'

Chloe nodded. She hopped off the bed and pulled her jumper and rainbow tights from under the covers, whipped them on before Ryan had the chance to turn his back, then strutted out of her room and to the front door.

'Well,' she said, holding out her hand to Ryan when he strolled up slower behind her. 'What are we waiting for?'

Laura paced back and forth backstage.

The Tandarah Community Hall was fast filling up. It looked set to be another sell-out. And what with the clever pre-show games, raffles and door prizes her favourite economist Ryan had lined up, it was set to raise almost double the amount they had raised the year before.

The cling-clang sound of old piano keys wafted through the curtains, and she wrung her hands as she went through her lines quick-speed in her mind.

She peeked through the curtains every now and then to see if her fan club had arrived, and when she saw the familiar strawberry-blonde moppet sitting in the middle of the fourth row she relaxed no end.

'Laura,' Ryan's smooth voice said from behind her.

She fair leapt out of her skin! Okay. So she wasn't as relaxed as she had imagined. Her hand on her galloping heart, she spun around. 'Jeez, Cowboy! Don't sneak up on a— Oh.'

Her diatribe came to a screaming halt when she saw Ryan standing before her in a black suit, a self-striped white button-down shirt and a lavender tie. Without the encumbrance of his now regular baseball cap, his dark hair made him seem raffish and dangerous. And he held a bunch of juicy red roses in his arms.

'You look gorgeous!' she said, unable to stop the words from spilling from her nervous lips.

'So do you,' he said. He was looking at her in a way she had not seen before, as if he wanted to tickle her, or strangle her, or…something. Her already nerve-ridden insides flip-flopped all over the place.

She managed a slight shrug. Blown away by the effort he had gone to on her big night, she was too tongue-tied to make coherent thought, much less a sensible sentence.

'I have a surprise for you,' he said.

'Um, could it be the bunch of flowers in your arms? Because I could pretend I hadn't noticed them.'

He seemed to only just remember they were there. His mouth twisted for a moment before he grinned at her. 'Nah. These are for some other actress.'

He placed the flowers on a card table at his side before reaching inside his suit jacket, pulling out a collection of A4 papers and handing them to her.

'What's this?' she asked, too full of nervous energy to see the words straight.

'It's Kardinyarr.'

Her nervously jiggling leg slammed to a halt as she stared at him. 'It's who—what?'

'Settlement came through at midday today. Kardinyarr

is all yours. Well, all Chloe's, actually. I have signed the property over into her name. With the proviso that the land is under our care until she turns twenty-one. I told you I'd been busy with farm stuff.'

Laura continued to stare. Kardinyarr. The guy had *given* her the home she had always dreamed she would one day be able to have for her daughter. The world beneath her feet wobbled precariously before the truth in Ryan's beautiful blue gaze brought her back down to earth.

'*Our* care?' she repeated, clinging to the words that had stood out the most.

'Well, I was hoping Chloe would let me stick around for a while. Build the place up to something really extraordinary so that she earns herself a nice little nest egg.'

'How long is a while?' she asked.

His heavenly blue eyes sparkled back at her as he said, 'As long as you'll have me.'

Laura knew the questions she was asking were only skimming around the issue. Was he really telling her he planned to stay? Or was she dreaming? She shook her head to clear the cobwebs. 'Are you sure about this, Ryan?'

'More sure than about anything I have ever done in my whole life. This is only the beginning, Laura. I plan to do a heck of a lot more to ensure Chloe has every chance in life. Every chance to do *whatever* it may be that *she* wants to do.'

Laura nodded. She saw the symmetry in his gift. He had never been able to be there for Will in that way. Never been able to give for the sake of giving. This amazing gift went a long way to healing that old wound.

Kardinyarr. Every square inch of paddock, of lantana

weed, of wombat hole, of splendid view, was to be in Chloe's family for evermore. Laura's dad would have been so thrilled. As would have Will.

She ached to bury her face against Ryan's freshly shaven cheek, to wrap herself in his warm arms, to leave this place and begin her life anew, knowing that Ryan really, truly planned on being there for as long as she would have him. And, if it was actually up to her, she knew exactly how long that would be. For ever…

Laura flapped the sheets of paper in front of her face to force back the suddenly brimming happy tears. 'Oh, no! You do realise that if I cry now this mascara is going to run all over my frilly white shirt and it will never be cleaned in time for curtain-up!'

'So don't cry,' Ryan said, and it was enough to make her laugh.

So, instead of crying, she did the other most natural thing in the world. She gave in to him completely. She threw herself into his arms. He rocked back on his feet to take on the kinetic wake, his arms reaching up to wrap around her so that the two of them didn't end up sprawled on the wooden floor.

His body was warm and hard beneath his lovely suit, and, wrapped close enough against him, she felt as if this was a defining moment in her life. Now *this* was a man who deserved her love, whether he knew what to do with it or not. The danger had dissipated; there was nothing but sanctuary in her foreseeable future—a future she could now see all too clearly with Ryan at her side.

'Hey, I'm not finished yet,' he whispered against her hair, his rumbling voice creating hectic shivers down her length.

She pulled away, making a big play out of checking

that her ruffles had not been squashed. 'More surprises? I'm still wondering who the roses are for!'

'Way more surprises than that,' he promised.

'What's next? Did you buy Chloe a condo in the city?' she joked. He smiled. She melted.

Esme, one of Laura's pirate gang, cleared her throat to garner their attention. 'Sorry to interrupt, Laura, but it's three minutes to curtain-up.'

'Thanks, Esme. Ryan was just leaving.'

Esme smiled pertly at Ryan. 'Not from what I hear.' Then she tootled off to hang out with the other cast members who had begun to spill onto the stage.

Laura blinked and dragged her eyes back to the man at her side. 'Sorry. Now, three minutes means you have more like five minutes—so quick. Spill. What's your next surprise?'

'My sisters are both here.'

Now, that was the last thing she had expected! 'What? Here?' she shrieked. She spun around, whipped open the curtains, her eyes madly scanning the audience. She found Chloe sitting in between two gorgeous dark-haired women who were both leaning down and listening to her excited babble.

'My parents would have been here too, but they couldn't get a plane out of Brunei in time. They're on their way and should be here in a couple of days.'

Unfortunately she watched too long, and Chloe soon found her peeking through the curtains. She leapt up on the chair, waved madly, and shouted loudly enough for Laura to hear the words, *'That's my Mum!'* echo across the large room. The two dark-haired women zeroed in on her and smiled. Beautiful smiles. Elegant smiles. Smiles full of perfect Gasper teeth.

Laura waved briefly, then shoved the curtain back into

place. 'Are you insane? I can't possibly meet them looking like this. And, oh, God! They're going to hear me sing! Even before I get the chance to wow them with my brilliant repartee, or impress them with my famous macadamia muffins, they will already have heard me sing! This is the worst surprise ever!'

Laura braved another peek, and soon realised that the whole row was in fact filled with dark-haired Gaspers. Gasper-in-laws. Gasper cousins. With her own little Gasper Somervale snuggled up in the middle of the lot of them.

'I wouldn't worry about all that, Laura.'

'Oh?' she shot back, hands on hips, staring him down. 'And why's that?'

'Your atrocious singing voice wasn't enough to stop me from falling madly in love with you.'

Of course the piano stopped tinkling, the cast members stopped twittering, and even the crowd seemed to fall silent at that precise moment. So Ryan's voice carried, his admission falling on at least a dozen pairs of ears apart from the one pair they were meant to reach.

Before Laura even had the chance to respond the Chinese whispers had begun. Before curtain-up, the whole town would know that Ryan Gasper, Will Gasper's brother, Chloe Gasper Somervale's uncle, was madly in love with their dear, sweet Laura Somervale.

'Could you repeat that, please?' Laura said, dragging her chin from its resting place somewhere near her chest.

'He is madly in love with you, honey,' Esme whispered, loud enough to set off a round of giggles in the front row.

'And his parents are coming into town,' one of the other pirate ladies repeated.

'To meet you,' Ryan joined in, his sexy grin focusing her on the subject matter at hand.

'And Chloe,' Laura said, going with the flow.

'And Chloe,' he agreed. 'But that could have happened any time they were next in town. I wanted my whole extended family to be here for the party.'

'Whose party? What party?'

'I wanted them to be here to meet you as soon as possible after I asked you to become my wife.'

'Laura!' Esme called out. 'One minute to curtain!'

Laura flapped a mad hand at her friend and co-star, hushing her loudly.

'That's it,' Ryan said. 'I've had more than enough of fighting for your attention. Come here, you.' Ryan grabbed her around the waist with one arm and delved the other deep into her hair. All Laura's hand-flapping and shushing was instantly forgotten.

'Laura, from the strength, emotion and honesty in your letter I was half in love with you before I even set eyes on you and on your beautiful corner of the world. But since I have come to know you I have fallen deeper and deeper every second. I adore you. You light up my world. Laura, you are my home. If you even feel half the love for me that I feel for you, I hope that you can find it in your heart to consent to become my wife.'

The music started up. The curtains ruffled. A sliver of light from the spotlights split the stage. And Laura couldn't have cared less.

'Oh, Ryan,' she said, before lifting up on her toes and, with her kiss, showing Ryan in no uncertain terms just how much she adored him. Her tears spilled in great running rivers down her face as she gave up every inch of her heart and soul to the beautiful man in her arms.

Ryan was the one who pulled away. A hand shielding

his floodlit eyes, he grabbed Laura around the waist and dragged her off-stage. When they reached the wings she was back in his arms, kissing him until she could barely think.

'Laura, though I would happily drag you all the way home right now, I fear the show must go on,' he whispered, his beautiful hot breath washing against her lips.

Laura pulled him back to her and kissed him to shut him up. The show could wait.

'I think I'm going to end up with more make-up on than you,' he murmured.

'So?' she murmured back. She was melting in his arms, and would have the chance to do so as much as she wanted for the rest of her life. What else could possibly matter more?

'Think of the poor drought-stricken farmers,' he said.

That was enough to bring her back to the present. 'Oh. You're right.' She pushed him away, sending him jogging down the steps beside the stage. 'I love you too, Ryan,' she called out.

'I know, sweetheart,' he said, before she slipped back into the darkness.

Ryan sneaked through the dark hall, then along the row of chairs until he reached the middle of the fourth row.

'I never knew *Pirates* started with a guy in a suit and the Pirate King locking lips,' Ryan's sister Sam whispered as she swapped seats with him.

'Well, now you know,' he whispered back.

Chloe heard his voice and looked up at him with a huge smile. If he'd thought his heart was full to bursting before, now he knew that it had more room than even he had expected. He grabbed Chloe and pulled her up onto his lap. She spun around so that she was looking him right in the eye.

'You love my mum,' she said. 'I just heard.'

Ryan could feel his sisters listening in intently.

'It's okay,' Chloe continued. 'I love her too. It's hard not to. Now, shush, here she comes. This is her best song.'

The Pirate King leapt onto the stage. Small, dainty even, and decidedly female. And the sexiest thing in purple pants Ryan had ever seen.

Laura sang her heart out. Her entire performance, every word, every song, she sang to him. Badly. Terribly, even. He had seen shows at the Met in New York, at the Arena in Verona, at the Opera House in Sydney. But never had he been so moved by any performance in his whole life.

He relaxed against the back of the rickety fold-up chair, his heart reaching out to the two women he knew would continue to surprise him and would continue to move him and love him for the rest of his life.

His girls. The Gasper Somervale girls.

0106/05a

MILLS & BOON®

Live the emotion

Millionaire's Mistress

In February 2006, By Request brings back three favourite romances by our bestselling Mills & Boon authors:

The Sicilian's Mistress by Lynne Graham
The Rich Man's Mistress by Cathy Williams
Marriage at His Convenience by Jacqueline Baird

Make sure you buy these passionate stories!

On sale 3rd February 2006

Available at WHSmith, Tesco, ASDA, Borders, Eason, Sainsbury's and most bookshops

www.millsandboon.co.uk